teeth

HANNAH MOSKOWITZ

SIMON PULSE

NEW YORK LONDON TORONTO SYDNEY NEW DELHI

SIMON PULSE
An imprint of Simon & Schuster Children's Publishing Division
1230 Avenue of the Americas, New York, NY 10020
First Simon Pulse edition January 2013
Copyright © 2013 by Hannah Moskowitz
For information about special discounts for bulk purchases,
please contact Simon & Schuster Special Sales at 1-866-506-1949
or business@simonandschuster.com.
The Simon & Schuster Speakers Bureau can bring authors
to your live event. For more information or to book an event contact
the Simon & Schuster Speakers Bureau at 1-866-248-3049
or visit our website at www.simonspeakers.com.
Designed by Angela Goddard
The text of this book was set in ITC New Baskerville.
Manufactured in the United States of America
2 4 6 8 10 9 7 5 3 1
Library of Congress Cataloging-in-Publication Data
Moskowitz, Hannah.
Teeth / Hannah Moskowitz.
p. cm.
Summary: "Rudy's life is flipped upside down when his family moves to
a remote, magical island in a last attempt to save his sick younger
brother, Dylan. While Dylan recovers, Rudy sinks deeper and
deeper into his loneliness." —Provided by publisher.
[1. Mermen—Fiction. 2. Supernatural—Fiction.
3. Cystic fibrosis—Fiction. 4. Brothers—Fiction.
5. Loneliness—Fiction. 6. Islands—Fiction.] I. Title.
PZ7.M84947Te 2013
[Fic]—dc23
2012019114
ISBN 978-1-4424-6532-9 (hc)
ISBN 978-1-4424-4946-6 (pbk)
ISBN 978-1-4424-4947-3 (eBook)

To my mom, who read me stories,
and my dad, who made them up

one

AT NIGHT THE OCEAN IS SO LOUD AND SO CLOSE THAT I LIE awake, sure it's going to beat against the house's supports until we all crumble onto the rocks and break into pieces. Our house is creaky, gray, weather stained. It's probably held a dozen desperate families who found their cure and left before we'd even heard about this island.

We are a groan away from a watery death, and we'll all drown without even waking up, because we're so used to sleeping through unrelenting noise.

Sometimes I draw. Usually I keep as still as I can. I worry any movement from me will push us over the edge. I don't even want to blink.

I feel the crashing building up. I always do. I lie in bed with my eyes open and focus on a peak in my uneven ceiling and pretend I know how to meditate. You are not moving. You are not drowning. It's just rain. It's your imagination. Go to sleep.

That pounding noise is pavement under your feet, is sex, is your mother's hands on your brother's chest, is something that is not water.

It's not working, not tonight. I sit up and grab my pad and pen to sketch myself, standing. Dry.

Sometimes the waves hit the shore so hard that I can't even hear the screaming.

But usually I can. Tonight I can, and it hits me too hard for me to draw. I need to learn how to draw a scream.

I close my eyes and listen. I always do this; I listen like I am trying to desensitize myself, like if I just let the screams fill my ears long enough, I will get bored and I will forget and I will go to sleep.

It doesn't work. I need to calm down.

It's just the wind.

Not water. Not anyone. Go to sleep.

Some nights the screams are louder than others. Some nights they're impossible to explain away, like my mom tries, as really just the wind passing through the cliffs. "Like in an old novel," she says. "It's romantic." Her room doesn't face the ocean.

Fiona, down on the south end of the island, says it's the ghost, but Fiona's bag-of-bats crazy and just because we're figuring out some magic is real doesn't mean I'm allowed to skip straight to ghost in an effort to make my life either more simple or more exciting. God, what the fuck do I even want?

I should figure it out and then wish for it and see what happens. Who the hell knows? Magic island, after all.

Magic fish, anyway. They heal.

That's the real story, that's the story everyone knows, but it's hardly the only one that darts around.

There are creatures in the water no one's ever seen except out of the corner of his eyes.

The big house is haunted.

Maybe we're all haunted.

I only take the legends seriously at night. The house is rocking, and the stories are the only thing to keep me company.

Stories, me, and ocean, and however the hell many magic fish, while my family sleeps downstairs and my real life sleeps a thousand miles away.

At home I never would have believed this shit. I used to be a reasonable person. But now we're living on this island that is so small and isolated that it really feels like it's another world, with rules like none I learned growing up. We came here from middle America. We stepped into a fairy tale.

And my brother is better but isn't well, so color me increasingly despondent, magic fish.

Out in the ocean the shrieks continue, as high and hollow as whistles. I get up and press my face against the window. My room is the highest part of our kneeling house.

The panes on my windows are thick and uneven. Probably the windows were made by hand. Even if it weren't so dark, I'd still hardly be able to see. Everything's distorted like I'm looking through glasses that don't belong to me.

But I can just make out the waves, grabbing on to the shore with foamy fingers and sliding back into the surf. I squint long enough and make out white peaks in the dark water.

"Go to sleep," I say.

I close my eyes and listen to the screams. I pretend it's my brother, my little brother, who has cystic fibrosis and this fucked-up chest and can't scream at all. Pretend this island has done the magic it was supposed to do, and he's okay. And we can go home.

It's just that at home there's so much green—trees and grass and Dad's rosebushes—and the water isn't ocean, it's what comes from the garden hose and the sprinklers and the fire hydrant when me and my friends pry it open. It's the sweat dripping down our faces. Home. We'd smoke cigarettes in the back of Abe's van, still soaked from the hydrant, and brag about the stunts he'd pulled. I'd lie to them all and tell them stories about the time I was arrested or my dad was arrested or, hell, that my baby brother was arrested. Back when he was just a two-year-old with a bad cough, toddling down the steps to chase us.

Home, before we had any idea how shitty this could get. When lung transplants and miracle cures were for other people.

Before we were desperate enough to believe, before we were a family alone in a dark room with everything crashing.

You'll cling to anything.

I fall asleep imagining I'm on a plane home. There isn't even an airport here.

two

WE HAVEN'T EVEN LIVED HERE TWO MONTHS, AND WE ALREADY have our routine down pat. My father stands in the gray granite kitchen, chopping potatoes and onions for omelets. Mom is on the balcony facing the ocean, my brother on her lap, hitting junk out of his lungs and letting the sea air slap them both awake. Two fish boil in the pot on the stove. Both for Dylan.

I trip over Dylan's rainbow xylophone on my way down the stairs. It's the only color in the whole house.

Dylan's talking a little; I can hear a bit of his voice drifting in through the open balcony doors. He must be having a good day.

"This thing's a biohazard," I say, giving the xylophone a nudge.

"I think it needs blood to be a biohazard."

"Nuh-uh."

"Trust me. I'm a doctor."

"I can straighten up. I'm not being a good kid, don't give me that proud face. I'm a useless shit and you know it."

"I never forget."

"It drives me insane. Fucking . . . stuff everywhere." I load my arms up with toys and cardboard books and my sketch pads.

Dad says, "Someday he'll learn to pick up his own stuff," and he smiles a little.

His hair is still damp from his shower. It's so humid here. We never dry. I try to shower as little as I can, because I hate being cold, and because there isn't anyone here I need to look nice for, anyway.

There's no one my age here, no one even close. There are two kids, around Dylan's age, both as sick as he is, if not sicker, though they've all been here longer so they're more hopped up on fish than the kid here, doing a little better. The next youngest person, after me, is thirty-two. She's here with her mother, who has lymphoma. I feel more camaraderie with her, when I catch her eye at the marketplace, than I do with anyone else here, my family included. I can tell she's here because she's obligated.

I don't think she's ever going to leave.

In two years I'll be in college. This will be the strange place I'll ferry to on summer vacation.

These three will go from my whole world to a picture in my wallet. That's how it's supposed to be.

I can taste it, and it doesn't taste like salt water.

Anyway, sometimes I wash my hair to look nice for my mom, which I guess is weird.

"How'd you sleep?" Dad asks.

"Recklessly," I say, just to say something.

"That was some storm. Wind was howling like crazy."

"Maybe a ghost," I say, because I like the way his face contorts. The fact that my father will not even consider a ghost reminds me that not entirely everything has changed. We are not entirely crazy.

I steal a piece of potato. One piece, a rough cube, cold and grainy. It splinters against my tongue.

I tug my hood up over my head before I step out onto the balcony. The wind hits me, cold and heavy, and I taste it underneath my tongue. Below us, Mr. Towner is strolling with his bag, handing out copies of the newspaper he prints in his attic. It never says anything we didn't already know.

Mom turns around and smiles when she hears me. Every morning she gives me this bright smile, like every morning she's surprised I'm still here.

I kiss her cheek, then Dylan's.

Dylan is twisting his shirt in his hands. His chest heaves up and down while he breathes. Each exhale wheezes out of his throat, like a miniature version of the screams that keep me awake. Even though his chest is tight, his breathing's pretty clear, because Mom just finished smacking him clean. When we first moved here, there was this instant, amazing moment of "Dylan is so much better"—but since then it's been slow. They warned us that would happen when we moved here. Get a cut on your arm and the fish will heal you right away, but my coughy little brother is still coughing.

"How's it going, short stack?"

Mom says, "I think he sounds a little better today."

Routine.

But he doesn't sound very good, and I can tell by the glance she gives me that he had a rough night. He has been better since we moved here, but there are still times we really, really worry.

Back home sometimes I'd stay up listening to him cough. I can't hear him anymore.

I give Dylan my fist to tap with his, and then he goes back to telling Mom, quietly, about the cartoon robot he saw on TV. I've never met a kid who cares as much about TV as Dyl.

I sit down next to Mom and zip up my hoodie. When I was a kid, I thought beaches were always warm. But it's only September here and I already feel frozen all the time. Something about the cold makes me want to pace all the time, but it drives my whole family crazy, so I try my hardest to keep still when I'm here and go for walks whenever I can.

"I need a heavier coat," I tell Mom.

She nods, immediately, and then more slowly as she keeps considering. "We'll have to order one," she says. There's a little farm here for milk and eggs and meat, but most other stuff rolls in on the slowest boat in the world. Like we did. Twenty days puking on a rocking boat, the opposite of immigrants coming to a better land.

"Ms. Delaney invited us all over for dinner tonight," she says.

"What about Dylan?"

Dylan looks up at me with those brown eyes. People usually estimate him as two and a half, which is almost exactly how old he was when we realized he was sick.

And the two and a half years of sheltering that came after mean that my goofy-ass little brother completely lacks social skills. My parents keep him cooped up because they're afraid someone will cough on him, but I do it because not everyone is as receptive to endless talk about octopuses and body fluids as we are, you weird kid, come curl up and tell me and leave the normal people out of it.

"Dylan can come," Mom says. "Maybe it will be easier to breathe, with the altitude."

"I think it works the opposite of that." I palm Dylan's head, and he makes this big show of trying to squirm away.

"It's only another hundred feet up, anyway," Mom says. "And she promised to show us a new fish recipe."

The rest of us usually only sample it, but Dylan eats nothing but fish—not just any fish, but *fish*, the kind people here mean when they say *fish*—technically Silver Enki Fish: fat glittery balls of scales that hide in the darkest water and under rocks in the marina. They're rare here but nonexistent everywhere else in the world. The Delaneys are the ones who discovered the fish, I'm pretty sure. Way back, decades ago, one of them was sick. And then they never left the island.

It's somehow still a fairly well-kept secret that the fish here keep people healthy, probably because it sounds so fucking fake. I had to lie to my friends about why we were going. I used the same lie people migrating here have used for generations—we think the sea air might help.

There's a reason seventy percent of the island's population is over sixty-five. This is a place for last resorts. The fish add years and years and years.

Being here is a good thing.

Dylan crawls off Mom's lap and onto mine. I let him stay until Dad comes out with breakfast. Omelets for us. Boiled fish for Dylan.

I eat as quickly as I can.

"Going for a run," I say.

Dad says, "Put some shoes on."

I have some mental block about shoes. I don't know. I'm always cold and I just won't put shoes on unless I'm forced to. I have no explanation. But I'm not going to put shoes on.

I stand up and Mom says, "Rudy, can you stop off by the marketplace, pick me up a bottle of milk?"

"Sure." I think she does that on purpose. Gives me goals. I like it.

I hop off our bottom step and make my way to the thick sand by the rocks, the damp stuff that takes a half second before it gives under my feet. The grains creep underneath my toenails. We are on the edge of the island and we have the longest walk of anyone to the marketplace, but we don't complain. My mom, I think, has this secret fear that if we piss anyone off, they'll stage an uprising and kill us, and no one will ever know. This island does feel like the perfect place for a murder.

I jog by one of my favorite places here—a long dock surrounded on either side by jetties of rocks. It's impossible to see if you aren't at a specific angle. My father fishes there sometimes, but he's never caught anything. There are tricks to catching Enki fish that nobody knows.

I think that dock is where the real fishermen used to work, but now they have a camp not far from our house, in the opposite direction of the marketplace. We hear them grunting and cursing at the fish and their massive nets, when the water isn't too loud.

The Delaneys' mansion sits above all of this, at the top of its dune, all its doors and windows shut tight. That house could be hit by a tsunami and never budge. Ms. Delaney rarely comes to the marketplace. I've seen her once. She has this guy who does the shopping for her. I don't think he's sleeping with her. He looks too happy for that.

The marketplace is only open on Tuesday mornings, and it's the highlight of everyone's week. A lot of the houses are clustered around here, the ones that aren't hideously cheap, like ours, or hideously expensive, like the Delaneys'.

The peddlers, who are just neighbors most of the week, but peddlers now, drive hard bargains as they hop from their stand to the others. The whole place sounds like the eggs and bacon frying at the farmer's station, and my mouth is almost shaking from the smell, but I don't have cash with me for anything but milk. I'm still not used to a world where credit cards are useless.

I nod at Ms. Klesko selling jars of jam and shake hands with Sam as he hands me a milk bottle. "How's your brother?" he asks.

"He's good. Eating well."

"Always a pleasure," he says.

Fiona the fortune-teller stops me with a hand on my arm

as I start to go. She looks at me, the wrinkles around her eyes deepening as she searches my face. I don't think Fiona touches anyone as much as she touches me. This should probably bother me more than it does. To be honest—and this sounds really stupid—I feel sometimes now like I'm actually starving for someone to touch me. God, it sounds even more stupid than I thought it would.

"The ghost is with you," she says.

I kiss her cheek so she'll let me go and then I head home, the bottle of milk cold and tempting in my hand. Halfway home, I give up and take a sip. Milk here is so heavy and thick. My mom used to tell me that milk was a food, not a drink. I never believed her before.

So I guess what I do is eat half the bottle. Mom is going to kill me.

To distract myself from the rest of the milk, I follow the path of the shoreline, looking for sand dollars. Today is too cold to even touch the water, but even when it isn't, I rarely go in past my knees. I'm not a strong swimmer. I don't think I've put my head under since we've moved.

Maybe I'll drop off the milk and then run more, blow off my schoolwork, go past my house until I hit the marina. I'll scale the cliffs. I'll watch the grimy fishermen catch my brother's meals.

And then I hear someone whistle.

I turn away from Ms. Delaney's mansion and that's when

I see him, sitting on a rock with a piece of seaweed hanging out of his mouth.

He's only about twenty feet from me. And before I notice anything else about him, I realize he's about my age.

And then the rest of him hits me: webbed fingers, the scrawny torso patched with silver scales, and a twisted fish tail starting where his hips should be, curling into a dirty fin. A fish. A boy. The ugliest thing I have ever seen.

Can't be real.

I take a few steps toward him, but I'm afraid to get much closer.

I'm afraid I'll wake up, I guess.

He gives me a funny smile and a small wave. And then he pushes off the rock and dives into the water.

I find him with my eyes a few seconds later. He's swimming out past the surf, hard. I see his fin hitting the water behind him with each stroke, setting up waves that push him farther and farther away from the shore.

He can't be a mermaid, because he has to come up to breathe. He's stopping to pant. He's tired. Mermaids sing underwater. Mermaids can't get tired.

Because mermaids aren't real.

And then he's gone.

three

"I THOUGHT SHE LIVED ALONE," I WHISPER TO MY MOM.

She holds her finger to her lips. I can't believe this. I can't believe that for three fucking months I've been thinking I was the only teenager on the island, and now I've found two others in one day. Even if one is half-fish.

I watch Ms. Delaney's daughter bring an enormous bowl of soup to the dining room table. Her red hair goes down to her hips. It sways with her like it's another limb. She's glancing at me, too. I feel guilty that I didn't somehow let her know I was here.

My parents don't look surprised at all. You'd think they would have mentioned her. Maybe they kept this from me on purpose. Maybe the whole get-your-brother-well thing is a ruse, and we're really here because my parents want me to be less of a slut.

At home I went to a school with over a thousand kids. I had strings of girlfriends and the kind of friends whose cars you borrow when you take them out, because theirs have bigger backseats. Here I do math problems alone at the kitchen table. If celibacy was their plan, it's working.

I reach next to me and rub Dylan's back while he chokes on his cup.

It's not like I actually think that's their plan.

Mom might not let me demand any more information, but she can't stop me from staring as the girl sits across the table from me and passes the mashed potatoes to her left. "Thank you, Diana," Ms. Delaney says.

Diana. That's also my mom's name. This never happens in movies.

My last girlfriend at home was Gabrielle. We were together for only a month before I left. I pretty much knew by the time we kissed for the first time that I was leaving soon. That's probably why I kissed her so hard that I bruised my lip against her teeth. I felt like I could get every bit of me inside of her, if I tried hard enough. I don't know.

We haven't written.

"I've never seen you before," I say to Diana.

"I don't get out much," she says. She sounds proud of it.

Diana Delaney doesn't seem like a real name, and she's so secret and pale, the closest thing to a ghost I've ever seen.

She's probably sick. There's got to be a reason the Delaneys stayed.

I turn my head and look out at the beach. Ms. Delaney has a window so big it takes up an entire wall. I'd be terrified, I think, living here with ghosts. They could push you right out through the glass and into the sea. You'd die with cuts full of salt water.

"This brie is phenomenal," my dad says.

Ms. Delaney slices neatly through her fish. "Linda Curlin, who lives down on the north tip? She makes it from Sam's milk, but of course it isn't available every week." She keeps chattering about the amazing apples she got from the marketplace last week, but while she makes small talk her eyes jitterbug from her plate and my parents back to her daughter, like she thinks any minute Diana will get up and run out the door.

Diana chews each bite of food a zillion times before she swallows. Her teeth are straight and perfect. Each sip she takes from her water glass seems to take a lifetime. I don't know how she does it. I want to shake her, or throw something at the wall. I at least get to go home to a house that isn't made of right angles and wade through my brother's toys. She stays here.

I want to take her by the wrist and pull her outside.

The conversation stays appropriately dull until Dylan faints, likely just from boredom, but my parents make a big deal out of scooping him up and making him drink water until he feels better. At home we're so used to Dylan fainting that we barely blink. Half the time he does it for attention. He's a clever little bastard. It doesn't usually work at home, but here at least it's something to talk about besides what fruit was good at the marketplace this week, so yeah, it looks like we're letting him get away with it.

Mom fusses over him for a minute, and Ms. Delaney murmurs "Poor thing" and "I hope he's all right." Diana looks kind of fascinated. Ms. Delaney is averting her eyes the way people think they're supposed to, like Dylan has an extra head and it's rude to stare, when, come on, he's five years old, he wants you to look at him. And Diana does, smiling at him like he's a little kid.

Dylan starts whining and reaching his hands out to me, so Mom drops him into my lap. I feed him fish off my plate and he keeps the fingers of my other hand trapped in his fist. It means only one of us can eat, but I'm not a big fan of the fish, to be honest. I've only had it a few times. It's expensive, and we need to save ours for Dyl. But the bit I ate tonight should beat off that cold I've been brewing, so there's that. I stuff all I can into the kid on my lap.

"Has the fish been helping him?" Ms. Delaney asks. She's still not looking at him. Diana nudges the salt and pepper shakers toward Dylan. I start to motion that he's fine, and then he grabs the shakers off the table and starts marching them like they're soldiers. Diana smiles.

Meanwhile, Mom and Dad are citing all the improvements in Dylan that they've only whispered to each other, like they're afraid getting too excited will scare it all away. (Dyl and I keep track of them and high-five and say everything out loud, thanks.) "His color's better," Mom says. "He doesn't get blue nearly as often as he used to, and chest percussion doesn't take as long. And we've even gotten a few words out of him. We've always had the hardest time getting him to talk, but now he's getting brave enough to use some of his air for that."

The Delaneys look at Dylan like they're expecting him to suddenly explode into the Gettysburg Address. Yeah, he isn't a trained monkey, and he *just fainted.* Give him a break.

He reaches for another bite of my fish, oblivious, and his back pushes against my chest as he breathes. He's not a great listener for a five-year-old, and we blame it on the breathing, but really I think he just acts like a bitch sometimes because he knows he can get away with anything. He flashes me that fucking smile of his. This kid can knock you dead.

He hands me the pepper shaker, and I play with him. He keeps knocking his shaker against mine like he's trying to beat it up, so I let mine fall over. He laughs, then coughs a little, and Dad glances over at me.

I apologize to Dylan, not to Dad, and rub a few circles on Dyl's back. He hides in my arm for the rest of the coughing, because we've fucking embarrassed him, fantastic. "It's okay," I whisper. "We'll go home soon." He relaxes a little.

Ms. Delaney clears her throat and says, "It really is amazing what the Enki fish can do. We came here when I was fourteen, when the cancer"—she waves the word away like it's a fly—"was close to killing me. My grandfather had written us letters about the place before he died, but we had no idea the effect the fish would have. And since I've lived here, I haven't been sick a day. My grandfather lived to be a hundred and sixteen."

My parents talk recipes and legends and I take advantage of the white noise and my brother buried deep into my shirt to lean across the table and say softly, "Is the other stuff true?"

Diana raises her eyebrows. "Is what true?" She looks much older than me with that look on her face.

I mouth *ghosts*, and she shakes her head. "Not ghosts like you'd think, anyway," she says. So I try *mermaids?* and her eyes widen, and she looks my age again.

The adults aren't listening to us. Ms. Delaney says, "And this is some of the best-quality fish we've had in a long time, this year. It's amazing the properties it has. I eat as much as possible."

"Me too," Diana says, but she makes a bit of a face. She

spears her fork through a bite of fish and turns it over on its end to rock-walk it across the table. "Right, Dylan?"

He sticks his tongue out the side of his mouth.

"Yeah, I know." She laughs, and he smiles.

I feed Dylan and listen to his chest loosen, and he looks up at me, like, "Am I well yet?" And sometimes it eats me up inside that I'm dying for Dylan to get well, but less for him than because I want to be done with our miracle cure and go home, and that makes me a really horrible brother.

"Where are you from?" Diana asks me.

"Michigan."

"Mmm. Like *Song of Solomon*."

"I haven't read that one. We did *Beloved* instead."

"I had a tutor for *Beloved*," she says. "He kept slipping up and saying Alice Walker wrote it. Wishful thinking on his part, I think. It would have been so much more subtle."

"Walker, um. *The Color Purple*?"

"Have you read it?"

I shake my head. "Do you have it?"

"I have eeeeverything." She rolls the word around the back of her mouth, and fuck, it's not like I didn't know I was easy before, but apparently a few months and a few smiles and the promise of a few books is enough for me to want to rip my clothes off right here at the table, parents and little brother and nice tablecloth be damned. Come on, Rudy.

Ms. Delaney is still going on about the fish. "They're getting harder and harder to come by. The fishermen are catching fewer every month, and they don't know how to explain it. They've been working so hard not to overfish; they keep their fishing methods secret to ensure they have control over the population. . . . There should be plenty. It's almost like the fish have discovered how to avoid the nets." She laughs, this high nervous thing.

"Maybe they're being hunted," Mom says. "We had a whole skunk population back home that—"

I say, "I saw something. In the water." Something covered in scales. Something that made Diana's eyes get big. "Maybe he's hunting them."

Mom says, "He?"

"Well, it. Whatever. It looked like a boy."

Ms. Delaney's head jerks up. "Where?"

"In the water. He had scales all over him." *He looked like he had a tail.* "He was a really fast swimmer. He looked, like, feral."

"Probably just a boy from the other side of the island," my dad says.

"He was a teenager. There are no other teenagers."

"What about me?" Diana says. But she's giving me a funny look, with her eyes narrowed. "A teenager? How old, would you say?" She looks like she's about to start taking notes for a news report.

"He wasn't really a teenager. He was . . . He had webbed hands, and—"

Then I see Ms. Delaney, as white as her fish fillet.

"Where was he?" she says.

"He was on the rocks by the big dock and then he—"

"How close to the house?"

I can't remember a time an adult has ever looked at me like I am this important. I wish I knew what the hell she wanted.

"Um. How close to this house, you mean? This house is on a hill. . . ."

She nods with every muscle in her neck.

"It was way down the beach . . . closer to our house than here. By the dock."

She looks relieved for half a second before she gets up and leaves the table. I hear her footsteps fading down the hall. We all turn to Diana for explanation, or help.

She shrugs a little and twists her face into a smile. "She's retired for the night, I'm guessing. Can I clear anyone's plates?"

My parents give me weird looks all through packing up Dylan and scraping plates into the trash, and I'm convinced they're wondering if the island has a psych ward for their son who sees merpeople until Dad nudges me and says, "Why don't you ask Diana over for ice cream?"

He's not nearly as quiet as he thinks he is.

24

I look at Diana "Oh, do you want—"

"My mother doesn't like when I leave the house," she says. "I don't think this would be a great night to test that rule."

"Oh."

"Some other time," she says, with a little head shake like she knows this isn't true.

"Huh," Dad says.

Dylan rests his head on my shoulder the whole way home. I keep one eye on him and one eye on the ocean, but I don't see the fishboy. Just my brother's head blocking most of my view.

Three nights later the screams outside wake me up from a soggy dream about Sofia, one of my friends at home, in a trash bag. It's a memory I'd almost forgotten—the time she got so drunk she passed out and we tied her up in a bag and tossed her in a Dumpster. We didn't go anywhere, just leaned against the Dumpster and laughed until she woke up. But we had no idea how freaked out she was going to be. She screamed and thrashed so hard we could barely haul her out.

I can look back at these things that I did and see that they were mean, but I don't regret them. They seem so far away, like they were done by someone totally different. And what I really feel is jealous that there was a point in my life—God, just a few months ago—where I could get away from all of this, run around with my friends, turn off my cell phone and not worry if my family would want me, and get all the human contact I needed from a drunk girl's leg as I folded her into a plastic bag.

And now the closest I can get to anyone outside my family is apparently a grip on the shoulder from a fortune-teller, a girl with my mom's name, and a series of piercing screams that may or may not be the wind.

And a fishboy on a rock.

I'm ripped from my thoughts about the screams by a different kind of shouting from downstairs. My mom to my dad. Those hurried, unsteady footsteps. He runs into something, curses. I don't hear coughing. That fucks with my head like you wouldn't believe.

I want to go straight downstairs, but it's so cold. I have to pile on socks—and I still want to be barefoot, what the fuck is wrong with me?—before I can let my feet hit the wood floor, and still it aches all the way up to my calves, like the time my friends and I dared each other to run barefoot across the frozen lake. And just like then, I'm not going fast enough, and I don't think it's possible for me to go fast enough.

Downstairs, Dad has my little brother tipped over his knee and he's hitting the kid's chest while Mom feeds him bites of fish and soothes him, and I don't know when she's going to figure out that those *"It's okay it's okay baby you're going to be okay's"* make Dylan more scared than he was before. It's how he knows when something's wrong.

It's so stupid, and I think I just do it for attention, but every time Dylan gets really bad, I feel like I can't breathe, either. I have to keep telling myself that my chest isn't closing up, that I can exhale whenever I want to.

I stick more fish in the microwave and try to catch Dylan's eye. "You with me, kiddo?"

"Yeah."

"That's my boy."

He pulls in this breath, this one breath, and it crashes through his lungs with more noise than I can make with my whole body.

Mom kisses his forehead. "That's right, baby. Great job."

I hand the plate to my mom and say, "What can I do?"

"Oh, honey, thank you," she says, like I caught the fish myself. Jesus.

"Dyl, you need anything? You have your dino—cool, you have your dinosaur. Okay. Cool." I blow on my hands. It feels like so much air. "I'm gonna go for a run."

Dad says, "It's the middle of the night, Rudy."

"No big deal. I'll be back soon. Okay. Awesome."

I just have to get out.

I'm just still so shitty at this.

I'm out the door without even putting on shoes. I'm running. The air has the rotted midnight smell of sea foam, and the sand is mushy underneath my feet. My socks are soaking through. I keep running.

I push closer and closer to the marina. There are no majestic sailboats here, just the dingy rowboats, one with a bell that I hear flapping in the wind on the most quiet nights, and the one corroded shrimp boat the fishermen must sometimes use. But I think they rely mostly on the big nets set up just off the shore that catch the fish as the current sweeps them around the corner, past the rocks. I've never seen anyone out in the boat.

It's almost four a.m., and I guess I thought the two fishermen would be awake by now, thought maybe I could barter a fresh fish or two off of them, but I only see one from here, lit up by the swinging lamp on the shrimp boat. He's . . . What is he doing? He's lying in the sand and . . . Is he on top of . . .

The fishboy.

I run faster. There's the fisherman. I can't tell which one; they look the same unless you're close enough to count the gold teeth. He has the fishboy just out of the water, in the sand, and he's digging his thumbs into the top of the fishboy's tail and biting his neck. I can't hear anything over the ocean.

So I yell, "Hey!"

They can't hear me, and now the fisherman is sitting on him, straddling his tail, rubbing his stomach. I'm close enough to see the fishboy's webbed fingers and his flailing fin and his open mouth full of sharp teeth. He gnashes, and the fisherman pulls his fist back and hits the fishboy across the face. I'm close now, close enough to hear, and it sounds like the time I stepped on a jellyfish.

I scream, "Hey!"

And at first I still don't think the fisherman heard me, but then in a second he's up and he's gone, disappeared into the shrimp boat without a look in my direction. And here I am, standing over the fishboy.

"Are you okay?" I say. And I feel stupid. I have no reason to believe this guy has a human brain in that human head.

He shakes his head hard for a few seconds and touches his cheek with his scaly hand. Then he sits up, balancing where his tail meets his torso, his fin curled behind him, and dusts himself off. "Thanks."

His tail is skinny and silver, the same color as Dylan's fish. All of his scales, especially the ones on his chest, look dry, like they're about to flake off. His hair is short and uneven. Mermaids in fairy tales are never this ugly.

Mermen.

I say, "Hey. All right?" Because his cheek is bleeding now, and because I don't know what else to say.

I should go.

"No. See, someone ripped off my head and gave me this stupid human one instead," he says. He spits a mouthful of blood into the water.

"Oh . . ."

"I'm fucking joking. I'm fine. Those assholes can never keep me forever, anyway. I bite. I would have gotten away. You didn't have to do that." He tries to scoot back toward the ocean, but it's obviously hard for him to move in the sand. "Hey. Give me a shove."

"I . . ."

"I'm not fucking contagious, I promise. And I won't bite you. Even though I could." He looks me up and down. "Yeah, I could take you."

I don't want to give him a push, because I don't want him to go. But how the fuck do I explain that?

I say, "What are you?" too fast for my brain to figure out what a completely shitty thing that is to ask.

But Fishboy just smiles and says, "I'm their dirty secret." He wiggles around a little until he's free, then gives me a nod and pushes himself into the ocean without my help.

I find a fish, already gutted and drying in the fisherman's basket, and run it home.

I really think I'll see Fishboy again. I can just feel it, in the hungry part of me.

So I'm holding my sick brother on my lap, keeping him busy while my mom fries up the new fish, and I'm thinking: My friends at home weren't nearly this interesting.

four

IT TAKES TOO LONG. I DRAW, I RUN, I DO HOMEWORK. I OVER
and over again think about going to Diana's and asking
about her books, or about . . . whatever. I chicken out and
reread the bloated paperbacks I brought from home and
watch the same five videos over and over again with Dylan.

I climb the cliffs by the house and think about climbing
trees in my backyard. I can't even remember the last time
I saw a tree. I'm trying to smell them in my mind, but all
I'm coming up with are the Christmas tree air fresheners.
That's not right.

I never pictured magic as this cold, gray, dead thing.

I climb all the way up to our kitchen window and tap

on it until my mom looks up. I just want to scare her, just to get some reaction, like I'm a fucking child, but she just waves like she was expecting me and, once I've hoisted myself onto the real land and through the door, tells me to sit down and do my homeschool work. Tricked.

She sits at the table with me and beats eggs while I scratch out quadratics on a sheet of graph paper. She has the baby monitor they use for Dylan pressed against her ear, like she's trying to use it to make a phone call. Dylan's down for a nap, so I'm barely a blip on her radar right now.

I tell her, "I saw Fiona at the market today."

Mom blows her hair off her forehead. "What are you paying attention to her for?"

Fiona tried to tell my mom's fortune once. She predicted a happy ending, and I think that's when Mom tuned her out.

"She was telling me about the ghost who haunts this island. Not even just Ms. Delaney. It's the whole island. Just one ghost, whole island. Whole ocean."

Mom says, "Really, Rudy," in this voice like she hasn't slept for days. Maybe she hasn't.

All the more reason she needs a good story. "It's the ghost of this boy they threw into the ocean who drowned. And now he just . . . wanders."

She looks up. "Why would you say something like that?"

This hits me like a slap in the face, because she's looking at me all fierce and angry and I wasn't expecting it.

I guess she doesn't like to hear about dead kids.

So I say, "It's not my story. It's just something she told me. I thought it was interesting. Come on, I'm not saying it's true."

She softens. "I'm sorry, Rudy. It's been a long morning."

"Yeah."

I feel like this exchange should help her unscrunch, but it doesn't. She's still beating the eggs, even though they're now all the same color. Her hand moves faster and faster. Her whisk keeps tapping against the bottom of the bowl. I have this thought that she's going to keep going forever, like a windup toy that never winds down. Like her whole purpose in life all of a sudden is to beat these eggs. She's done all this shit for me my whole life, and now all I can imagine her doing is beating eggs.

When I was a kid, I always felt like I needed to keep her safe. She was made of marshmallows and candy canes and she knew twenty hundred lullabies. Dad would give me these talks about how we needed to protect her, and I would feel like a knight. And I loved it. I loved every wimpy bone in my mom's body, because I felt so fucking strong.

Now she's made entirely of steel, and Dad's the one who cries every time any little thing is wrong. And Mom never cries. She hasn't cried since the first time Dylan was hospitalized. I can't decide if I'm afraid to see her cry again, because of what it would mean, or if it would be a relief, like coming home. I don't know.

The house creaks in the wind.

"Your father wants to take you fishing," Mom says.

I wonder how hard Dad would cry if he dipped his fishing line in the ocean and pulled out a ghost.

Or a boy.

Maybe I'm thinking about this all wrong. Maybe the fishboy is the ghost.

I should have touched him. I missed my chance to find out what he was.

A ghost is as good a guess as any, I suppose.

And now I'm focusing on the fact that my father is trying to schedule time to be with me, acting like Mom is his secretary, and that feels even more unbelievable than a fishboy or a ghost. We used to play Ping-Pong in the backyard. We used to split peanut butter sandwiches.

I say, "Oh. Okay. I guess I'll talk to him."

She nods tightly, like she's afraid if she moves any more, her cheek will slip, for even a second, from its home against the baby monitor.

"How's Dylan?" I ask.

"Sleeping well."

"Good." I wonder where Dad is. He probably went for a run. We used to run together. There's no reason, not a single good reason, why we don't anymore. It's like my barefoot thing; I want it to mean something and it just doesn't.

The ancient clock on the wall clicks with each second, but the hands are so springy that every click has two tones.

I've got this glass of water that just tastes like salty air.

The clock is making me fucking crazy.

Mom gets up and goes to the stove. I say, "Mermaids can breathe underwater, right?" I don't know. Because I have to say something. Because I want her to have answers.

"Rudy, do your homework."

"Yeah, but—"

"Stop procrastinating."

"Can you look at me for a second?"

She turns around and does, of course, with this soft expression. I guess I'd forgotten that she still looks at me like that. I thought she saved all those looks for Dylan. I didn't even pay attention. God, I can be a callous asshole when I want to be. And I want to be all the time, it seems like.

I wish Dylan were up from his nap. Lately he's been really into playing pirates, and I could go for that right now. Someday maybe Dad and I can build him a real boat, just a tiny thing, and I could take him out on the water, and we could look for—

Oh. The fisherman was touching him. He couldn't have been a ghost. The fisherman had his hands all over him. The whole thing was . . . God. I don't want to think about it.

Besides, I don't even know why someone would think

about doing anything with anyone who looks like the fishboy, and it's not like he could do anything more than kissing, since he's scales and fins from the waist down.

"How do you have sex with a mermaid?" I say.

"Rudy, *honestly.*"

"Okay, sorry. God." But I don't know if she even hears me, because she's holding that monitor like she wants it to be a part of her skull. And I don't even know if I'm sorry.

I draw that night, with Dylan watching, with enough of my attention on the waves instead of the page that it takes me a really long time to realize I'm sketching Diana.

Not a good idea, Rudy. One girl on a whole big island. If you're not going to marry her, stay the hell away.

I drift off that night imagining regaling her with stories of my conversations with the fishboy. I dream up a smile for her.

five

MOM AND DYLAN END UP COMING WITH US TO GO FISHING, which should probably make me angry. But really I'm thankful that we can blame the awkwardness between us on Mom's presence rather than the simple fact that we have nothing to talk about. "How's a guy supposed to bond with his son with a chick around, huh?" Dad says, with a wink at me, and I smile back. After that, we don't know what to do.

It's not that we don't have anything in common. It's that we have everything in common, and every single bit of our lives has been discussed to death, and neither of us has anything to say that won't put the other to sleep.

But Dylan is being adorable, sitting next to Mom in the

sand next to the dock, kicking his feet in the spray. Mom keeps worrying that he's going to get loose and float over to us somehow and we're going to catch him with our fishing lines. Sometimes, the things she finds to worry about, it's like we don't have any real problems.

"We're going to catch the freshest fish you've ever eaten, Dyl," Dad calls down. Dylan could not care less.

But I'm getting comfortable sitting here on the dock, with just the tips of my toes freezing in the water. For a minute everything really is okay. I get my brain to shut up, and I breathe. Dylan digs in the sand until he finds a sand crab, one of those massive armored bugs, and he goes absolutely wild and shows it to Mom, laughing so hard he starts coughing. She's nervous watching him get all worked up, but she's smiling, too.

It's warmer today than it has been, and even though the sun's starting to go down, I'm not shivering for the first time in what seems like forever. I could probably convince myself that it's summer, if my goddamn feet weren't so cold.

I look up at the Delaneys' mansion, or what I can see of it, anyway—the stilts, the underside, a bit of the lowest balcony that juts out over the dune. I don't think they could see us unless they really craned over the edge of the balcony, which is probably a good thing, since none of us has gone up to the mansion since that time I ruined dinner two weeks ago.

I see a pair of legs—in jeans, sneakers, Diana—on the mansion's deck, facing away from us. This might be the first time I've ever seen someone whose gaze doesn't naturally aim at the ocean. Whenever you have a conversation with anyone here, their eyes are always drifting toward it, like we're all compasses and the whole sea is north, or like if we look away for a minute, we're afraid it will disappear and nothing will hold us here. We'll forget why the fuck we're on this island.

This is the first time I've seen Diana since that dinner. And it's the first time I've ever seen her outside. I keep expecting Ms. Delaney to come and call her in, to tell her she's going to catch a cold or something.

I wish I knew what the hell was up with them. Maybe Ms. Delaney believes the ghost story, and she's afraid of them, and afraid for Diana, so she keeps them both cooped up. Maybe Ms. Delaney met the fishboy once. Maybe she's not a fan.

Diana might be able to see us now that she's on the sand and beyond the crest of rock that stands like a fence in front of her house, so I go back to scanning the water. I'm hoping the fishboy will appear, even if just to prove to my parents that I'm not totally crazy. And it would probably impress Diana. I'd look like some superspy, spotting the mysterious sea creature before anyone else.

But when I check back toward the house, Diana is gone.

I see the curtains inside move and the hint of her hair as she draws them closed over the huge window.

An hour later we still have no fish, and Mom thinks it's time to pack it up and go home. "I'll make brussels sprouts," she says, like this is an incentive for us to hurry up. Or maybe she's just rubbing in our failure. We're so lame, we have to go back home and eat soggy brussels sprouts instead of fresh fish.

A big wave crashes on the rock in front of us. It misses me but soaks Dad. And I laugh until he yanks me up a few inches by the back of my shirt and threatens to throw me in the ocean. He tugs me up to kiss the top of my head and drops me right before his fishing rod almost jumps out of his other hand. "Hey," he says. "Got something."

"Hallelujah," Mom mumbles, pulling yet another sweater over Dylan's head. Soon we're not going to be able to identify him. We'll think he's a pile of laundry.

Dad's fishing rod jerks with another sharp tug, and then he says, "Shit, feels like I lost it." He keeps reeling in the line.

My own fishing rod tugs. "Whoa, Dad, I think I got something now."

"You have it?"

But then my line jerks and lets go the same way his did. "Lost it."

"What the hell?" Dad holds the end of his fishing line in his hand. Both the bait and the hook are gone. What's left of the end of the line is frayed like someone sawed through it.

Or like someone bit it off.

I reel my line in as quickly as I can. The same.

"What the hell happened?" Dad says.

"Mm. We must have got them caught on the rocks and the bottoms pulled off. Cheap line?"

"Must have been . . ." He looks at Mom suspiciously.

Then Dylan starts to cough, and he's hacking up shit that a kid his size shouldn't have the ability to hack up, and Mom says, "We'll have to solve the mystery of the fateful fishing trip some other time. Inside, all right?" Dad agrees because he has to.

I say, "I'll be in in a minute."

"If you miss dinner, you're getting skinned." Sometimes my mother reminds me she's from the South.

"No such luck. Skin Dyl in my stead."

Once they're gone, I toss my fishing pole into the sand and walk to the end of the dock. I don't see him, so I chance it and yell, *"Hey!"*

I worry for a second that Diana's going to hear me. Then she'll really think I'm crazy. Yelling at no one.

But Fishboy says, "Hey yourself."

I turn around, and there he is, just his torso bobbing out of the water, his arms crossed over his scaly chest. He has the broken ends of our lines in his mouth, hooks dangling by his chin. "So what the fuck was that?" he says. "You save a fish from the big bad fisherman, then you stick fucking hooks in the water to try to kill all the rest of them? What the fuck kind of joke is that? And I thought you were interesting."

Um. "You're a fish?"

"What the fuck do I look like?"

"Fiona says you're a ghost."

He laughs once. "Fiona's full of shit." He spits the hooks into his hand and buries them in the sand. "She said Ms. Yves would die at a hundred and two. I heard someone say yesterday that she's a hundred and five. So."

"You know Fiona?"

"I know all of you." He smiles. "Rudy."

I take a step back.

He stops smiling. "Is this really a surprise? What do you think I have to do all day? Spy on all you fucking humans while you kill the fish. Yep. Great. Thanks a lot."

I can't stop watching him while he talks.

He says, "Are you gonna be a fisherman when you grow up, Rudy? They don't even have to do anything, now that they have those fucking nets up; it's like, they can sleep all day and kill the whole population." His face is turning red while he talks. "God, you're even worse than them, you know? Because you walk around with your cute little family like you're so fucking whatever, then you come down here

42

and start hunting all of us. Yeah, you're such a little hero, saving the one fish and going home and eating a whole father-whatever-baby set for dinner."

"What the hell is wrong with you?" Maybe he likes fish so much that he fused himself with one. Maybe that's what happened. That doesn't make any sense. "You're not a fish," I say. "You have, like, hair. And arms. Lungs."

He seems to be agreeing with me, if a little reluctantly, until I gesture to his chest, and then he grabs me by the legs and tackles me into the water.

I'm not fast enough to close my mouth, so I taste everything: the salt, the algae, the shed scales. I never realized before how loud water is.

And mother of Christ, it's cold. I struggle. The fishboy's hands keep gripping my thighs, hard, like he's trying to tear them off.

It's the longest anyone besides Dylan has touched me since I've been here.

I'm kicking and it's not working shit it's not working. I'm going to drown. I can't believe I moved to an island without learning how to swim. I'm choking and I'm going to die. . . .

He's pulling me down as hard as he can, and he's going to kill me, fuck, my parents are going to actually fall apart, but one of my flailing feet nails him in the ribs and it startles him enough that I can scramble to the surface for a breath.

My foot brushes his tail. It's rough and ugly like a rash.

I push myself away from him, panting, grab on to the edge of the dock, and pull myself up, into the air. Safe. I'm huddling against the wood like it's my mother. I don't know if I'm strong enough to haul myself back onto the dock, so maybe I'll just stay here forever. This is my new home.

He's panting too. Probably from the kick in the ribs. He was already pretty bruised.

I say, "You're not a fish, you're a fucking maniac."

He laughs, hard, his face up to the sky. I see all his teeth. There must be a hundred of them, as thin as pine needles. He has a loud, piercing laugh, like a whistle.

I know that voice. He's the screams at night. He's the hours of screaming and the crying that my parents told me is the wind.

Goddamn. Either he really is a maniac, or he's got to be the saddest fishboy in the world.

He grabs me by the front of my shirt. "I don't want to see you around any more dead fish, you got that?"

I pull myself back. "My brother needs them."

I really didn't think this would concern him, but he lets go and looks at me. He keeps his eyes narrowed. "What's wrong with your brother?"

"You're a shitty spy."

"What's wrong with your brother?"

"He's sick. Cystic fibrosis."

"Cystic whatever." He doesn't say it mean, but like he's trying to figure out what I said. "Whatever fibrosis." He tilts his head and I practically see the words rolling around in his brain. It's not an uncommon reaction. It's *so normal.*

I say, "Yeah. The fish are making him well."

He pushes his tongue into his teeth. "They're working?"

"Yeah." Slowly.

"Well. Good, I guess." There's this pause, and then he goes, "The little one, right? Who was with your . . . you know."

"Mom?"

"Yeah."

"That's the one."

The fishboy rubs the back of his head. "My hair used to be really long. It was awesome. Fisherman cut it off, said I looked like a girl."

"Oh."

"Your brother's cute. How old is he?"

"Five."

I can tell he doesn't like this answer. "Oh. He looks more like four. I thought maybe four."

The way we're balanced in the water right now, I feel like he's a lot shorter than I am. And his frown makes him look suddenly younger.

"Good luck with that, then, I guess," he says.

I say, "Thanks."

"But stay the fuck away from my fish."

Wait. "I . . ."

Fishboy mumbles, "Sorry about your brother," then he pushes off from me and swims away. He's faster than I could ever be, but he doesn't get out very far before he stops. His silver-spotted chest is heaving. I should have kicked him somewhere.

Then he dives back under the water and he's gone, and I psych myself through a few breaths *(can let go, will not drown, can let go)* before I let go and push myself off the dock and hold my breath until I hit shore. I walk home shivering and trying to think of what story I'm going to tell my parents about why I'm all wet, but when I get there, Dylan's coughing so hard that they don't even notice me come in.

six

TWO DAYS LATER I'M CROSS-LEGGED WITH MY SKETCHBOOK when I hear Mom climbing the wooden stairs to my room, every one of her footsteps creaking the house closer and closer to the demise I've imagined and drawn a thousand times. I've been drawing a lot since I've been here. My friends and I made it a point to berate each other for any hobbies that didn't involve girls or cigarettes, so my books and sketch pads were kind of contraband back home. Now it's like when you have your favorite meal every day for a month. Too many drawings. She knocks on the open door of my room, and I'm really grateful for an excuse to stop.

She and Dad have been fighting all day. I don't even think

it's about Dylan this time. Just like Mom looks for things to worry about, they search for stupid reasons to fight. I guess it makes them feel more normal.

She comes in and sits down at the foot of the bed. I like my mattresses thin and firm, which baffles Mom. She hates sitting on my bed because it reminds her that I'm sleeping somewhere she would never tolerate. She says she feels like Harry Potter's aunt. Another example of making up problems where there aren't any.

"Wow, look what you've done with the place." She grins while she looks around the room. I've taped a few of my pictures up. It's not much, but it makes the irregular walls look more uniform when they're all papered with my sketches. "I like that one of your father," she says.

"The one of you with Dylan is the best. I got your noses perfectly."

She kisses my forehead and hands me a letter. "This came for you."

Everyone here is really crazy about mail. People are always leaving cards and letters in each other's mailboxes. We got all these "Welcome to the island" notes when we first arrived. Everyone gets excited when mail arrives from the real world, too, since it can take almost a month for the boat to bring it to us. That must be why I haven't heard from anyone at home. Their letters just haven't reached me yet. I can't believe I thought they were blowing me off. Here it is, here's proof that they didn't all forget me. I used to get an e-mail or a Facebook message at least every once in a while, and I know it's my own fault for not answering—but what could I even *say*? I would need to invent a real location, a real school, a real life—but I still wasn't expecting them to dry up this quickly and this completely.

Mom's gone, and I still haven't opened the letter. I'm staring at it, clinging to it like a raft in a storm. I know it's stupid, but I feel like I need to savor this moment. I let myself believe, just for a second, that the letter will say someone has found a loophole, that I get to come home. That ever since I left, they've been scheming ways to get me back to my house and my school and my life.

It's going to tell me that everything has paused since the second I left, and nothing has changed, and my girlfriend misses me, and there's a set of lungs for Dylan, and none of this has even happened. And that fish don't do magic and they don't talk.

I turn the letter over and look at the return address to see which one of my friends its from. And it says just "Diana."

I hiss air out through my teeth. Goddamn it.

Rudy—
I am locked in my tower, awaiting your rescue.
But I'll meet you at the door.

My mother typically cries in the bathroom most Tuesday nights, on the opposite end of the house. For your peace of mind.
Perpetually,
Diana

This is just great. This is exactly what I need in my life right now.

I want to get back under my quilt and sleep for a million years.

Although, in my admittedly limited experience, if a girl tells you her mother isn't going to be around, it means she wants to have sex with you.

So I should be twitching. This should make me feel . . . something.

I've been stuck in one place for way too long. I don't feel anything. All my thoughts these days are either profound or profane with nothing in the middle. Nothing normal. I'm contemplating the sea or I'm contemplating jacking off. Maybe sex is the answer.

It's touching someone, at least.

And it'll give me something to do on Tuesday, something to do besides listen to the screaming ocean, or finish my math problems, or draw more pictures of my brother or my parents or more of the ones hidden under the skinny mattress, the ones of girls from home with their shirts off and the ones of the fishboy and his healthy lungs and his tail. That's something. It's just something.

Dylan's a fiend with puzzles nowadays. So even though it's cold and almost dark, he and I are out here on the deck with all the pieces spread on the picnic table, because the puzzle's so big there isn't room for it inside.

Dad's looking through the doors periodically and smiling at me, like it's praiseworthy that I'm playing with my little brother, I don't know. Sometimes I think they forget who I am and what makes me happy.

Dylan doesn't solve puzzles like normal people. He concentrates on one piece at a time, always, like if he stares hard enough at it, he's going to see the whole puzzle. Once he's looked at a piece long enough, he sets it aside and starts over with another. And I'm chuckling at him, trying to fit two pieces together. Then he makes some noise of triumph, and I look up and he has half the puzzle finished over there. This kid is great sometimes.

Sometimes I wonder if he remembers before he was sick. It sounds horrible, but he was somewhat of an unremarkable part of my life then. I was crazy about him when he was a teeny baby and cuter than sin, even though I had to pretend that I wasn't, because I was eleven and stupid. But then he got to the bratty toddler stage, and that's when I was starting to spend more time out of the house, too, and he sort of became just an annoying blip on my radar, except when he would crawl onto my lap all sleepy and smelling like orange juice, and that part was okay. My parents worried about why he caught every cold and why he wouldn't put on weight, but I didn't, really. Worrying wasn't my job.

And then practically overnight he stopped being a kid and became a walking tragedy. He's the world's smallest ghost.

He finds the piece he was looking for and holds it up with both hands. I say, "Good job, buddy," and his face is like I've just fixed the whole world.

seven

ON TUESDAY I SCAN THE WATER ON MY WAY OVER TO THE MANSION, but there's no sign of the fishboy. And once I've climbed the hill and the huge doors open up, he kind of flees from my mind. Diana opens the door in a very serious black dress, all of her hair piled up on her head. "Thank you for coming," she says, in a voice I imagine a butler might use.

Then she grins, and the bridge of her nose wrinkles, and I realize she isn't fully delusional, she isn't some let-me-show-you-the-world lost girl and she isn't Emily Dickinson with a sex drive, she's just a teenage girl fucking with me, and it's been so long since I've been around anyone my age that I didn't even recognize it.

Really, if she had sent a letter that said, *Hey, want to hang out,* would I even have come? Probably weirding me out was the right choice to get me here.

"You're a tactical genius," I tell her, shutting the heavy door behind me.

She says, "Don't go thinking I'm all normal just because I know how to get what I want. I can get unfortunately batshit. It's not cute. Make sure you're not expecting cute. This isn't *Looking for Alaska.*"

"What will your mom do if she finds out I'm here?" This is dirty talk, and I think she knows it.

But she just shrugs. "Probably nothing. But let's pretend." She grins. "I'll give you a tour."

That's another code phrase I know. It means, we're going to my room. This is going to be the easiest sex I've ever had. I don't know how I feel about that.

Diana is leading me down this wide hallway with walls stacked with portraits. They're so old and dusty that they almost look velvet, like those hideous pictures of dogs my grandmother has in her house in Tampa.

Diana says, "I hope you weren't expecting me to show you around our splendid homeland."

"Why don't you leave the house?"

"Occasionally I do. It isn't usually an option."

"Oh."

"It makes my mother worry. And most of the time I don't

want to. Everything worth it comes to me eventually. There are a lot of things out there I don't need." She looks at me, her eyes slightly narrowed. She reminds me of the fishboy for a second, with that look on her face. "You wouldn't understand."

No, after three months of dying to get away, I don't think I would.

But then she says, "And everything I want to know I can read about," and it's like a string yanks out of me and ties itself to her. She nods toward an enormous library as we walk past. It's so stupid, but the way our hands linger the same way on the door frame, for a minute I feel like I can understand everything about her.

Books. Books I haven't read with spines I don't recognize. I want to go in. I want to sink into one of the gold armchairs and smell the dust from all the pages. I've read our house's measly collection of waterlogged paperbacks four times each. Please. Please can we stop.

But we keep walking. I try to pull myself together. I've missed both books and girls, but I don't think this is the time to try to bargain my way into both.

I realize it's warm in here. I shrug out of my raincoat. Diana takes it and drapes it over her arm.

I say, "Oh. Thanks."

"'Course. I've always liked raincoats. I like weather-specific clothing."

"And you don't go outside."

"I also like Turkmenistan and I don't go there either."

"I have a weird thing with Argentina."

"The bottom line is, there is a world outside waiting to kill you, and my mother has experienced more than enough of it for both of us."

Whoa. "What happened to your mother?"

"A horrible injustice," she says. "But a fascinating one. My room is right through here."

She leads me in and shuts the door behind her. There aren't any chairs, so I sit on the floor, leaning against the bed. It's thin and gray, just like mine. This whole room is blank and pale, and the only accents are the stacks and stacks of books.

She moves her hands to the top of her head, twists something, and all her hair falls down to her shoulders. I think there's glitter in it.

Her room smells like peppermint.

"Overwhelmed" seems like the wrong word, but it's all I can think of. And I think there's something wrong with me that what I most want to know right now is more about her mother. God, Rudy.

But she walks to me and sits down next to me on the rug. "I find you very interesting, Rudy," she says.

"You do?"

I find myself really boring, most of the time.

She says, "I haven't seen a teenager since Elizabeth Danziger used to babysit me. And I didn't pay attention then, and she moved away years ago. And I've never seen a teenage boy before." She stares into my face. Her eyes are so light blue they almost look white. "I've only seen pictures."

"You're really freaking me out," I say, but I whisper it. Because her lips are so close to mine.

She grins.

But then she's kissing me.

Her mouth is warm and soft. This feels more like drinking hot chocolate than kissing. Her lips and her tongue are everywhere, filling my entire mouth, and it's suffocating and it's a little fantastic.

It's not that I've been an angel, and it's not that I don't like Diana all right, but I don't think I've ever kissed someone I cared this little about. Here in this room, we could kiss, we could have sex, she could kick me out, her mom could discover us, and it wouldn't really mean anything. Nothing would change. It's not as if my life needs her.

There's something freeing about it, and no amount of thinking can change the fact that I'm sitting here, my hand on her waist, her hand in my hair, with the unfleeting thought that I want her to swallow me.

And it's so warm.

We kiss for a few more minutes—hours, in kissing-time—

but I don't get bored. I could keep doing this until we fall asleep. But she pulls away, rests her forehead against mine, and says, "Very good."

Man, she's a good kisser for a hermit. I say, "You must read a lot of books," and she laughs.

"Just the right ones. I special-order them!"

God, I wasn't supposed to get caught in this trap, she fucking warned me, and now all I'm thinking is that I want to bring her outside, somewhere farther than the bottom of her house or the marketplace. I want to take her off this island and run away with her to Argentina.

Christ, I'm so easy. A girl kisses me, and all of a sudden I'm making plans to elope with her or some shit. I need to cool down.

While I'm taking even breaths in and out, she says, "So far this is nice," in a voice like she's making the decision for both of us. Which is fine with me.

So I say, "Thank you."

"Do you have a lot of experience with girls?"

"You sound like you're writing a report."

"I'd never read about sucking the bottom lip like that."

"Yeah, one of my . . . My ex-girlfriend taught me that."

"Hmm."

"Did you like it?"

"I didn't mind it."

"Well. Thanks."

I look around her room, at the stacks of books on the floor. Most of them are old ones I haven't read. The only classics I've read are the ones for school. I feel like I should ask her how *Jane Eyre* ends, because I never finished it.

"You like books?" she asks. Kind of gently.

I nod. I can't look at her right now, for some reason. I'm scared she's going to ask me what my favorite is, or like she won't believe me, so I say, "Roald Dahl." I say, even though she doesn't ask, because I can feel the question sitting between us anyway, because I feel like I have to prove myself. "I like Roald Dahl. Um. I read them to my brother." Not true, but it's easier than explaining that I like kids' books more than adult books, or reality.

"*The Witches*," Diana says, with a nod.

"*Fantastic Mr. Fox.*"

She stretches out on her stomach and puts her feet in the air, her ankles twisted together. I remember flopping like that when I was a kid. It makes her boobs look amazing. She says, "I like how his books pretend to be about something for the first third, then switch gears completely."

"The real plot doesn't show up until the middle, yeah. And usually the real characters."

"And everything before that is completely dropped." She smiles and rolls onto her back. She's basking in this conversation. "It's like a little story of its own that's never finished."

"Only Roald Dahl could get away with that shit. I mean, they let him write *The Magic Finger*." I take her copy of *Runaway Bunny* off the bookshelf. "I like that you have this in here."

"Picture books are my favorites."

I am so warm. "This is a war metaphor, my mom told me." I look at all the illustrations, the rabbits with their soulless eyes. "Like, sending your kid off to war."

"It's about sending them off anywhere, really."

I don't know how she got so close to me. Her lips are right against my cheek, all of a sudden, and I turn and kiss her because I don't know what she's going to say next, but for a second, I can feel all her thoughts about books, all these possibilities, hovering between her lips and my cheek. And I want to taste them.

Like sandalwood and dust.

She pulls away faster this time, but she smiles at me more.

"We'll do this again," she says. "But my mother will be recovering from her crying jag soon, and I don't think she wants to see you after she humiliated herself in front of you at dinner."

"Why's she afraid of that boy I saw?"

"So it is a boy."

"You know about him." It's a statement, not a question.

"As much as I care to know about anything in . . . the ocean."

God, the way she says "the ocean," I half expect to hear lightning crashing in the background.

She says, "My mother doesn't talk about him, but I know things she doesn't expect. And I've seen your boy a few times. I don't think he knows I can see him."

"He stays by the dock, I think. He's not my boy."

"I can see the dock if I angle myself just right on the balcony. I don't think he hides as well as he thinks he does. But I wasn't quite sure he was a boy, with his skin. I couldn't tell what he was. A boy?"

I shrug a little. "He's not a fish."

"He doesn't have any legs."

"Why was your mom humiliated?"

Diana rests her forearms on each other. "Long before I was born, my mother liked to consider herself the kind of person who would try anything. I've stumbled across tales from her wayward youth. All these men she's bedded." Diana looks over her glasses at me. "All these nonmen she's bedded."

"Your mom's big secret is she slept with women?"

Diana coughs in the back of her throat until she turns it into a laugh. "Broaden your mind, Rudy. You just saw a half Enki, didn't you?" Then her face gets a little more serious. "Why do you think we're afraid of the ocean?"

"You don't seem afraid."

"Do you ever see anyone swimming?" She shakes her head

and plays with the pristine cover of *Runaway Bunny*. "We can't kill off those fish fast enough, really, if you ask me."

"Wait. What are—"

She smiles. "If I tell you everything now, what will make you come back?"

Well.

You will, for one.

eight

THE FOURTH TIME I SEE FISHBOY, HE SCARES ME OUT OF MY MIND.

Except it might not really be the fourth time. Ever since he cut our fishing line, I've thought I've seen glimpses of him every time I step outside, and a few times I'm sure I've seen the tip of his fin or a bit of blond hair poking out of the water. Even when I look through the thick bottle glass of my bedroom window, the ocean so blurry I can't make out the peaks of the waves, I think I can see a hint of a tail weaving in and out between the rocks. Diana's right. He's a shitty hider. It's almost like he's trying to be seen.

Although, now that I think about it, I don't know why he really cares if people see him. He's clearly not hunting the fish—he's the very opposite of hunting the fish—so I don't know why everyone would be so bothered to know he's in the water. And if he's eavesdropping on us all the time, he must get sick of people calling him a ghost. It must suck for people to think you're already dead when you're not.

He must get so fucking lonely.

So why does he hide?

And why didn't he hide from me?

And if he doesn't want to reveal himself to us, I don't know what he's doing here. If I were him, I would swim so far away from this island. But he's always here, lingering by the dock and the cliffs.

He still ducks under the water or underneath the dock when he sees anyone approach, so he's clearly not waving his presence around like a flag. But now that I know he's here, I don't understand how I lived here this long without seeing him. I don't understand how he's only a legend to everyone on this island, why they don't try to talk to him, or catch him. Not to hurt him, to touch him.

Except then I go to the marketplace and see them obsessing over any new rumor they can imagine up, and I get that they don't spend more time trying to verify them. They move from thing to thing too quickly. Last week a rumor went around that Ms. Klesko cheated on her husband, and it swept us all up like a hurricane. Even my parents were talking about it. For the week it was like Ms. Klesko's affair was the only thing in the whole world.

How could they really care about a fishboy when they're worn out from caring about each other?

So what's wrong with me?

I don't want to make this corollary.

The fishermen know he exists. There's that. And for some reason they haven't told anyone. They shrug their shoulders when they don't bring enough fish to the marketplace, but they never try to blame the ghost. I listen to the fishboy scream at night and don't know why they don't kill him. They'd rather catch him and beat him up every night than be through with him for good?

The only person who seems to really want to know anything about our little ghost is Diana, and I haven't seen her lately, because we haven't had a Tuesday, and she hasn't sent another letter.

The real fourth time that I see the fishboy, the time that counts, I'm looking for him, under the guise of looking for sea glass, when I find him a million or something feet away from the shore, just a blur in the distance. But I can see him struggling in the water, panting, coughing. Coughing hard.

I drop my sea glass and stare at him. I can feel my heart all the way down in my bare feet.

He coughs something into the water, something that my

experienced eye tells me is blood. His shoulders heave down as he's breathing, and I can see his bottom half moving frantically to stay above water as he coughs.

And I'm frozen on the shore, just staring. Useless.

Of all the ways for this fucker to die.

And I can't go help him. It's not even a possibility. He's way too far out. And even if I got to him, he'd probably annihilate me with those sharp teeth, since he thinks I'm a fish killer.

If he can even get the breath to annihilate me. Because right now, I don't think he even has the oxygen to look at me and realize that I want to help. I do, I really do.

He keeps coughing. I think he's choking, even though I know that when someone really chokes, there's no sound. Just dead quiet and huge eyes.

I'm too far away to see his eyes, but not too far away to see him starting to slip under the surface of the water as more blood spills out of his mouth.

And he can't breathe underwater because he's the worst fish in the world, and even if he could, he's coughing too hard to get anything in, and holy fucking shit holy shit—

A huge wave crashes in front of me, and I jump back. When the water rushes away, the fishboy is gone.

Shit.

I climb onto the dock and run down to the end to try to see him. Nothing.

"Come back come back come back," I whisper. "Fuck. Get up. You're a fucking fish. Stop drowning." It's like everything in my little world depends on whether or not the fishboy comes up for air. And he isn't. He isn't coming back.

And something inside is screaming that I don't want anything to happen to him. And I know it's selfish. And I know I need to stop caring about people just because they make me feel better about my life. But right now it's what motivates me to dive into the water, so I'll take it.

The water rushes up my nose and into my mouth. I try to open my eyes. The salt stings me like acid. I'm going to die before I even get to him. This is awesome. This is the worst idea I've ever had, and the ocean is wrapped around my neck to strangle me.

Relax. I come up for air, not because I need to, just to prove to myself that I can. Breathe.

Swim. I shove myself off the dock with my feet and fucking flail as hard as I can. I'm not moving fast enough. I'm breathing too much because I keep getting scared and worrying that I'm not going to get another breath in. I'm not going to get there, and the fucking fish is going to drown. I kick my feet with everything in me.

I only know when I reach him because my body collides with his. He's still completely under the water, his arms and chest curled around his tail.

I reach an arm around his waist and pull him up. He's

a lot lighter than I thought he would be, or maybe it's just buoyancy in the salt water. Either way Fishboy feels even more breakable to me than he did the other day, with the big eyes.

I kick hard until both our heads are above the water, but his face is still frozen and shut, his cheek resting half on his shoulder and half on mine. And he looks like shit. He has a red and purple bruise from his cheekbone to his eyebrow, cuts and bruises all over his shoulders, a blue boot print over his rib cage. Christ, if I'd been beat up this badly, I'd be coughing up blood too.

"Wake up," I say. "Christ, wake up." The water's too deep here. I can't tread water for both of us. We're both going to drown. Shit.

I don't even want to know what Dylan would think of me if I died like this.

Just as I'm starting to sink, Fishboy coughs water and his eyes flutter open. "Fuck." He tries to pull away from me for half a second, but then he stops and holds on so, so tight. His voice is hoarse like Diana's. And he's still clinging to me, his fingers wrapped around my arm.

"Holy shit, what happened?" he croaks.

"Coughing." He doesn't know it, I don't think, but he's holding me up now. "You got dizzy."

"How long was I underwater?"

My chest is starting to ache from breathing so hard. "Forever."

˙ "Yeah. I wish." He pushes away from me and shoves his hair out of his face. "Thanks."

"No no no. Now I'm going to fucking drown out here."

"Calm down." He pushes me toward the shore. "There's a sandbar about twenty feet that way. Rest there until you're ready to swim back."

"What about you?" I say. He's still totally pale. Except for that bruise, and the blood dripping out of his mouth.

"I'm fine."

"Bullshit. Did the fishermen do that to you?"

"What the fuck do you care?"

"I just swam all the way out here to save you."

He grins. "I'm like your pet." That smile kind of catches me in the throat. I didn't see that coming.

But all I can say is "Shut up," because I'm starting to sink under the water again. Buoyancy my ass.

"Okay, I got this." Fishboy takes a handful of my soaked shirt and swims me to the sandbar. Sweet fucking Jesus. I lie on my back and pant for a while. I don't know when the water stopped feeling so cold. Now that I can breathe, I feel like I could stay here forever.

He stays on the edge of the bar, where the water's a foot or two deep, and he sits and scrubs sand off his fin, watching me. "You all right?"

"Yeah." I stand up and catch my breath. I'm towering over him now.

He clears his throat. "Anyway, thanks again. Bye."

"You're going?" The shore still looks impossibly far away.

He says, "I have things to do."

"Bullshit. You just lurk around the dock all day."

I expected this to make him mad, but he shrugs. He got mad about having lungs but not about this? "I do things."

"I've saved your life twice now."

"Yeah, just in time for me to drag your sorry ass back to shore."

"Not to shore, apparently."

"Poor Rudy."

"I think I should at least get your name."

"Who says I have a name? What do I need a name for? All the fancy parties I go to, yeah? I need to whatever and drink wine and introduce myself." He sips from an imaginary glass.

He has a point.

"Fine." I don't know why I'm so disappointed. I guess I really wanted a name. It would make him more real.

But then he sighs. "Aw, look at your face."

"What?"

He says, "Teeth, okay? My name is Teeth."

Even though I almost just died, I'm laughing. "What kind of a name is that?"

He doesn't smile. "The kind I gave myself. What kind of a name is Rudy? The kind your parents gave you?"

"It means 'famed wolf.'"

Now he grins. And I'm still smiling, too, so it's kind of like, for a minute, we're the same.

I guess that's a stupid thing to think. I look down at his hands. They're so webbed they're practically fins themselves, and they're so much smaller than mine.

He makes this big dramatic sigh. It's this ridiculous relief to hear him breathe. Then he says, "So I guess this is the part where we stop acting like this is the last time we're going to see each other."

I tilt my head a little and look at him. "Huh."

He rolls his eyes. "I'll see you around." He smacks my cheek gently. His hand is rough, freezing cold, and doesn't feel quite alive.

"Sure," I say.

He rubs the back of his head. "Look at this. I have no fucking hair. Fucking fishermen. I told you this, right? They said I looked like a girl with it long."

My eyes slip down to his chest. I'm picturing Diana's. "You, um, don't look like a girl."

He shrugs. "I don't care. Girls are fine. Girl fish."

I wrinkle my nose.

"I'm kidding. What am I going to do with a fish?" He turns around slowly, showing himself to me. "I got nothin'."

I feel like I shouldn't look. "Well . . . you look like a boy."

"I'm a fish. You're going to need to accept this. I'm a fish."

He messes with his hair again. I really don't think he likes how it feels. He says, "So you can get back to shore okay?"

"Um, yeah."

And then he's gone.

The part of this where I'm really scared out of my mind doesn't come until I'm back in the house, tucked into my room, trying to get warm under the covers. I start thinking about the fishboy—Teeth, freezing cold Teeth—turning blue in the water, coughing and wheezing, and then bitching about his hair a minute later, like it's nothing, like it happens all the time, maybe. All of a sudden I'm shaking so hard my teeth are chattering again. And I can't get warm, no matter what I do. I'm just shivering like a nightmare.

nine

I'M TRYING TO DO MY HOMEWORK AT THE KITCHEN TABLE, BUT Dylan really wants me to play with him, and to be honest, I want to play with him, too, but Mom is giving me these hideously dirty looks because I was supposed to have all of this finished two weeks ago. So I have to give Dylan a hug and an "I'm sorry, buddy."

I wave my math problems at my mom. "I'm doing these outside," I tell her. To get away from Dylan. Yeah. That's the only reason. Definitely the only reason.

I go straight to the dock.

I'm only lying there for a few minutes before he bobs out of the water. "Hey."

I try not to look surprised. It's been a few days since the rescue with not a lot of signs of him, and I guess I didn't think that of the two of us he'd be the one seeking the other one out. Maybe I didn't really think I was going to see him again unless he needed more saving.

I'm getting used to the look of him, at least, with his flaky scales and his millions of bruises. He's like Dylan's hideous stuffed dog that started looking cuter the longer he carried it. "Hey," I say.

"Aren't you cold?"

I shrug. What am I supposed to say, *Yeah, but I was hoping you'd swim up?*

"What are you working on?"

"Math." Avoiding the essay.

"I can do addition."

I look at him.

"I'm very smart," he says.

Still, I don't know where a guy like him learns addition, or where he even learns the word "addition."

"Mm," I say. "Not addition, though."

"Let me know if any comes up."

"Will do."

He leans his elbows onto the dock and watches me work. Then he sinks under the water, and I think he's gone for good, but a few seconds later he pops up behind me on the other side of the dock.

"What are you doing?" I ask him. He's back beside me again, this time with his elbow right next to mine. I watch him out of the corner of my eye while I scratch answers. He smells like a fish, I'll give him that.

"Keeping an eye on you."

He reaches out to touch the page, then stops and wipes slime and water on my sleeve before he starts tracing the numbers as I write them. After a minute he turns his attention to the lines at the top of the page. He traces the date, which I still write on top of everything, out of habit, then puts his finger on the word next to it. He writes the letters with one finger, trying and failing to curl up the rest of his hand. The webs between his fingers stretch so thin.

I stop working and watch his finger. He's left-handed.

After a minute, he says, "Rrrr."

"Hmm?"

He's staring at the top of the page. "Rrr. Ruh."

Oh.

"Ruhd," he says, after another minute. He's frowning hard, the skin wrinkling between his eyes.

"Rudy," I say, kind of gently, I hope.

He's quiet for a minute. Then, "Oh."

"Where the fuck did you learn how to read?"

"I can't read. You just saw me not reading."

"Someone obviously taught you something."

"Go away," he says, in this small, angry voice, the exact

same one Dylan uses when he wants me to think he's mad at me but he really isn't. It doesn't work any better for Teeth.

I say, "You know, if you want? I can teach you to read."

He studies me for just a second before he scowls and dives back into the water. He's really gone this time. He splashed my page, and now the ink is all smudged.

I'm on my way home when I see Diana under the house. She's craning her neck to try to see the dock from here, but she can't. "Were you with him?"

"Not just now."

"It's very cool that you know him."

"You should come meet him sometime."

She shakes her head hard.

"Have you ever even been to the ocean?"

"It's rough."

"You don't have to go in. Or you can go out past the waves." I say this like it's no problem, like I do it all the time.

She looks at me like I'm about Dylan's age. "I didn't mean that kind of rough."

"Um . . . oh." I don't know what to say, but she seems done with this conversation anyway. She pulls a book out of her bag and hands it to me. A copy of *The Metamorphosis*. I would have read that this year, if I were at home in my real school.

I don't know if she always carries books or if she was

waiting for me, and I don't know which I want to be true.

"I think you'll like it," she says. "We'll discuss later."

God, it shouldn't get me this turned on that she keeps acting like she's older than me. Especially considering she has my mom's name.

But then she's kissing me, and I don't care what I'm supposed to think for a few minutes. I still don't know about her, really, but I know I like books, and I know I like kissing, so this feels right.

And now, for a few reasons, my routine has changed.

I still hug my family when I wake up and still watch Mom hit Dylan's chest. Every day but Tuesday, when Mom still sends me to the market and my nights take a different sort of shape, I head down to the dock. Fishboy and I don't say anything about it, but he's always there now. It doesn't feel like he's waiting for me, and it doesn't even feel like I'm going there to see him, most of the time. It's just like we happen to be at the same place at the same time.

We don't always talk much. He'll show off his new bruises or the rips in his tail. He'll tell me stories about what the fishermen do to him that I hope to God are exaggerated. The stories always end the same way. "And then I bit them and got away."

My price for getting to listen to his stories, according to him, is that I have to learn how to swim rather than kind of flail around. "I'm not going to be whatevers with someone who can't swim," he says.

"Whatevers?"

"Yeah, like friends or whatever."

He never looks at me when he's talking. His eyes are always scanning the ocean and plucking out Enki fish; I can't believe how easily he finds them. He holds them and cuddles them and lets them go, usually in the opposite way that they were going. "They're so stupid sometimes," he says. "They'd swim right into the nets if I let them."

"You're like the fish protector," I tell him, and that seems to make him happier than anything I've ever said.

He claps his hands together. They make a noise like something squished.

"Swimming," he says. "You have to learn to swim."

He says the most important thing is that I learn how to float (*I can fucking float*, I say, and *Reliably*, he says, so whatever) so I spend a lot of time lying on my back past where the waves break, my hairline tipped into the water, kicking, while he bitches about my flexed feet or the way I'm holding my shoulders. Every conversation we have gets easier, and it amazes me over and over that there's someone here I can talk to without agonizing over every word, because finally there's someone who sounds more like a belligerent idiot than I do. Even back home that was hard to find.

"Hold on." He leaves me floating on my back while he

rescues some fish who got stuck in the current and are about to be swept over to the nets. He can't rescue nearly all of them this way, but he does what he can, cradling each one in the crook of his elbow before he lets it go. "I don't usually see them actually get caught in the current," he says. "I've only really rescued three today. The others I just said hi to."

"I'm sinking," I say.

"Well, stop." He swims up to me and puts his hands underneath my back. He lifts me a little. "Up."

I go up.

"Good. Not sinking, see?"

I try to nod, but I'm scared to move my head.

After a minute, he says, "So."

"So?"

"So what's cystic whatever?" His voice is very, very neutral.

"It's this disease in the lungs and the stomach. He coughs and he gets infections and he's really thin . . ." I try to explain, but it's a lot harder than it used to be. I can't just recite everything that's the matter like I used to, listing everything he can't do like I'm reading off a menu. Because the truth is, Dylan is getting well.

And that's the other part of my routine that's changed. Because every morning I hug Dad, I kiss Mom, and Dylan shouts, "Rudy!" and springs off Mom's lap and wraps his arms around my legs. "Puzzle. It's really important." Sometimes he has to pause and take a shuddery breath between words, but he keeps going. "Play with me."

Sometimes I do. But it's kind of terrifying, because it's like the whole world for Dylan when I stay and put together a bit of his puzzle with him. I worry that I'm actually doing him a disservice by playing with him. I'm just multiplying his broken heart the day that I go off for college or go back home or drown or something, and the last thing this kid needs is a broken heart.

"Pay *attention*," Teeth tells me. He sounds like someone's mom. "You're floating away. Kick."

I kick, but I can't get back to him. He has to come fetch me and drag me back to the dock. "You are so annoying," he says. "You're like that bunny sometimes."

I laugh. "What?"

"The runaway one."

I try to sit up and plunge right through the water.

Sometimes in the afternoons I take Dylan out to walk on the beach with me, though I still carry him for most if it. My hips are always sore by the time we get home.

"Can I swim?" he asks me.

"Nah, it's way too cold." This seems like an answer he can understand. It's easier than telling him that there's no fucking way I'm letting his head go under the water. Mom still watches him like a hawk whenever he's in the bath.

Then he says, "No, can I?"

Oh.

I look at him and kiss his forehead. "Maybe someday."

"Probably?"

"Sure, probably."

I think I see Teeth out in the water. I wave Dylan's hand at him.

"Who's that?" Dylan says.

"My friend." We can't see Teeth's tail from here, so he looks almost normal. Plus, I can trust Dylan. The kid's good people.

Dylan waves on his own. Teeth waves back. I see him bring his hand to his mouth to chew on his fingers in that way he does.

That night my door creaks open. I'm not asleep. I'm listening to the screams and wondering if the fishermen have Teeth again. Maybe there's another reason he screams. Something not so bad. I don't know. It's too early. They shouldn't have him yet. I don't like this.

He hasn't told me how often they catch him. He doesn't usually get specific about that, and he laughs so hard about it during the day that it can be hard to believe the screams are really his. But I know his voice by now. I recognize it when it's scraping against his throat and breaking into sobs, even though I've never heard him sound that way unless it's night, like this, and everything is blurred out by the noise of the ocean.

I sit up. Dylan's standing in my doorway. He's breathing hard and loud.

I say, "Did you just climb all those stairs?"

He nods.

I don't know if it's more amazing that he did that all on his own, or that Mom and Dad have clearly turned the baby monitor off because they know he's okay at night.

Magic fish. Another scream cuts through my ears.

"Had a bad dream," he says.

I'm about to go over and get him, but then he runs right up to me and pushes into my arms.

He is so warm and soft and real.

It's not just because I have this scrawny fishboy in my life that he's not the skinniest thing in the world anymore. God. Dylan. Just fucking Dylan, okay?

And then Teeth screams really hideously, and Dylan has his face buried in my neck, and I start crying, so hard that I can't even believe it, and my fucking five-year-old brother is holding me and telling me, *Don't cry, it's okay, it was just a dream, you're awake now.*

And I can't stop crying for anything in the world right then. And I can't let go of him. Nothing could make me let go of that kid. The house could fall into the sea and crush everybody and we could go underwater and I would hold him the whole time.

ten

THE NEXT TIME I'M WITH DIANA, I CONVINCE HER TO LET ME
into the library, finally. I think she was bluffing when she
said her mother wouldn't care that I was here, because she's
all anxious as we enter and quietly close the doors. "She's
right there," Diana whispers, pointing through the wall, and
if I listen very carefully, I can hear her crying. The noise is
familiar in a way I can't place.

Diana collapses in a plush armchair with a copy of *The
Wind in the Willows*, and I drag my hands over the shelves,
skimming the spines. I walk past a hundred books I'm dying
to settle down with. I finally find what I want in the back
corner of the library, closest to where Ms. Delaney is crying.

I grab this battered thing, this scrapbook, and sit down next to Diana. She barely raises an eyebrow when she sees what I have. "Detective work?" she says.

"I figured your family would have something written down."

"We did discover this place." She doesn't sound nearly as proud of this as she did about never going outside.

I pour myself into the papers and start reading. These are letters, articles, and journal entries, all handwritten and dated from fifty years ago. Something in me crumples when I realize there isn't anything newer.

I shouldn't care. I'm here to read about the fish, anyway. And I do. I find out more about the fish than any of the townspeople have been able to tell me. The scales can be poisonous, they can probably see just as well as we can, but they're weak swimmers. They mate for life.

They've been known to attack humans. God. I should say no to Teeth next time he asks me to swim. He's lucky they aren't attacking him. But I think of the fish I've seen, as round and lazy as tiny balloons, their scales the same dirty gray as Teeth's tail. They don't look at all capable of attacking a person. And I don't know why they would.

There used to be tons of them, which was why the Delaneys started eating them in the first place, when really they had actually come here for the sea air. And, well . . . the rest I mostly know. The papers use the world "balance." The fish make you how you are supposed to be.

So eating them wouldn't cure my Pinocchio of a friend into a real boy, I don't think. I guess I'd wondered.

There aren't any scientific reports here. There isn't a reason why.

But there's no reason to think that the effect wears off. There's no way to know, since anyone who needs the fish, as far as I know, hasn't stopped eating them. The only people who ever leave this island are the ones who were here for a family member, who eventually cut free, or leave when their mother, a hundred and five years old, long cured of cancer, dies peacefully in her sleep from nothing but a tired body.

And I'll leave and my parents will eventually die, and my brother, my little fucking brother, is going to be stuck here forever. We'll have drilled it into his head that the most important thing is surviving and maybe he'll never even think that if the only way for him to do it is to live here alone and hopeless and go slowly crazy and so old. Maybe he'll never move back to the real world and wait for that lung transplant. Maybe he'll marry Diana. Maybe he'll die alone.

Before I leave, I've really got to introduce him to Teeth for real.

Or . . . fuck. Maybe I can't leave.

Just . . . just *fuck*, okay?

I put the papers down on my lap.

"You seem disappointed," Diana says. But she's not look-ing at me.

"Just thinking."

"Nothing about your fishboy in there, huh?"

"Uh-uh."

"Yeah, all that is in my mom's diaries." She turns a page in her book. "His exciting conception."

I'd kind of figured, but I wasn't expecting confirmation to be that way. "Half-brother fish?"

"See why I prefer books?"

"Where are the diaries?"

She chuckles a little, her eyes still locked on her book. "Not in here, I'll tell you that."

She's not going to tell me. Goddamn it. I groan and flop backward in the chair. She's still grinning.

"Have you read *A Farewell to Arms?*" she says. "It's good."

"No."

"I'll lend you a copy."

"Thanks." But I can't pretend this is what I want. Half an hour ago, books were all I wanted. Now I want a fuck-ing boat. Someone to offer to ship fish to the states. An actual cure.

"He is getting well, though." I'm sitting on the dock, throwing pieces of seaweed into the water.

"That's kind of why you're here." Teeth scoops his lips

over the surface of the water and gobbles up the seaweed I threw. I toss the next piece into his mouth.

"I guess I didn't believe it would really happen. You know I could bring you some real food, right? Candy, even."

"I hate human food." He's eyeing the seaweed in my hand. "Give me the rest of that."

"There's more everywhere. Go get your own."

He whines, long and loud, like a scream. "That's a really good piece. You got lucky."

"Or maybe I picked it out on purpose. Best seaweed in the sea."

"Stop fucking around. It's not like you need it. You can't even eat seaweed." He stumbles around the word a little.

"Of course I can." I eat a bite to screw with him. It just tastes like salt. "How often do the fishermen catch you?" I say. I've been trying to get him to talk about them all morning. He has this bruise around his neck in the shape of a hand. And his eyes are really red today.

"Most nights. They're crafty."

"I don't get why you don't swim away."

"I just bite them. So you guys are going to stop eating the fish now, right? Now that he's well."

"We don't eat them, really. Only him."

"Is he going to stop?"

"I don't know. I don't want him to go back to how he was. And it's not like he's totally well."

"I think it's time to stop, Rudy. I mean, what if . . . what if he becomes whatever from the fish from eating too much?"

"Uh, allergic?"

"No."

"Immune."

"Jesus Christ, if I knew the word I'd fucking say the word, Rudy."

"All right, kiddo, calm down. It's not like we're eating you."

He sighs, really big, in this way that reminds me how much of him is human. I can hear all the air leaving his lungs.

"Stop being mean and give me that," he says, pointing his chin at the seaweed. "All I ever do is skim the shit off the surface. Dead and slimy. The good stuff's too hard to pick."

"You're really not adapted to your environment."

I mean that as a joke, just more banter, but he kind of looks away and splashes a little with his tail.

I say, "Hey, I'm sorry."

"I'm not exactly . . . whatever. A thing that was made for what I do." He's doing the *whatever* thing the more we talk, because I guess we're venturing past the subjects he's used to hearing about. He learned English from listening to the islanders, I assume, and if they don't say the word *evolutionary*, he's not going to know it. It's not like there's anything for him to read out here in the ocean. Really, he's the opposite of Diana in every single way, ever.

"I'm a mistake," he says. "Let's be honest."

I want to ask now about his mom. If he knows she's still up there in the mansion. And how long he was with her. And if he remembers when she must have read him *Runaway Bunny*. And about how the hell one goes about having sex with a fish.

He pushes himself out of the water to try to get to my seaweed. He snaps at the air. His teeth are long and thin as needles. I pull my hand away before he can bite my fingers off, and he says, "I'm not going to *hurt* you."

"I know, asshole."

"Plus they're sharp, not strong. I probably wouldn't even break skin." He bites his hand to test and examines it critically.

"Stop that. Like you're not beat up already."

"Didn't break skin."

"So your bullshit about biting the fishermen is actual bullshit, then. Do they just let you go?"

"Why the fuck don't you ever get in the water unless I'm giving you a fucking lesson? You're driving me crazy. Jesus. Get in and give me that."

"I'm not getting in today. Water's rough." I remember when Diana said that.

"Then why are you wearing a bathing suit?" God, he sounds just like a bratty kid sometimes. All of the time.

I say, "Because somehow or another you seem to always get me in the water. But I'm not fucking coming in voluntarily. Go out and start choking again if you want me in so badly."

He grins. "So many big words."

"Sorry."

"I liked it."

"Not coming in. Will freeze."

"Scared you'll drown?"

I say, "Yeah," before I process that he was probably teasing me.

But I am. Maybe not as scared as I am that every time I get in the water I will keep getting closer to *this is your life, this is your friend and you are never leaving,* but I'm not telling him that bit. Kid doesn't speak English, he wouldn't even understand. Yeah.

He looks at me for a while, then pushes off the dock with his fin and floats around on his back, beating the water with his tail. He has even more scaly patches on his chest than I remembered. I swear he's the ugliest thing in the world. And the bloody hole in the middle of his tail is glistening.

He says, "What if I show you something cool? Something *life-changing.*"

I say softly, "Why do they put holes in your tail?"

He ignores that. "Something really cool, Rudy."

"Can I fix it?"

"What?"

"Sick brother. I have the fix-it impulse."

"Show you something."

"Yeah, fine. How cool?"

"Really, really cool. But you can't tell the fishermen. Promise?"

"What? Do you really fucking think I'm having conversations with the fishermen?"

"I never know what you humans are gonna do. I'm not a very good spy, remember? Come on. I'm not going to let you drown, God, I'm a fish."

"You're not a fish." I slide into the water as slowly as I can, feeling like all my limbs are going to snap off from the cold and my balls are going to jump up into my body. We're past where the waves break, but the peaks still smack me in the face on their way to shore.

"Why do you keep saying that?" He waits until I'm halfway into the water before he grabs me by the shoulder and starts pulling me out to sea.

"Holy crap. You're murdering me."

He gnashes his teeth and laughs, and I can't help it, I'm laughing too, although I'm still worried that while Fishboy is trying to show me something cool, the sea is going to swallow us both alive. And, in all honesty, sometimes I still worry. Sometimes he feels too charismatic to not be a bad guy. He's a little too much like I was at school for me to completely trust him.

But then he'll smile at me, and sometimes I don't really give a shit whether he's bad or not, as long as I'm not bored. And I haven't been since the first day I rescued him.

He drags me over to the marina. "Don't be seen," he says, and he latches on to a rock and peers around it to the fishing docks.

"Seriously, let's get out of here. This is bad." Why the fuck does he even come here? Shit, I don't want to watch them beat him up. Do they even beat him up during the day?

"Uh-uh. Come here." He pulls me to a new cluster of rocks. "Okay, here, dive down and open your eyes."

"I can't open my eyes underwater."

"Do it anyway." And he dunks me under the water.

I take a few seconds to convince myself that I'm still alive, and then I open my eyes. It hurts. Of course it hurts.

But then, fish.

Hundreds of them, all around me, swimming and nudging each other and screaming—I can't believe it, actually screaming—in the same high-pitched voice that has become my lullaby or my nightmare or something.

Teeth is beside me. He grins.

I stay down for as long as I can, and then I come up, gasping. Fishboy emerges a minute later, one of the fish in his hands.

"This must be like a colony or something," I say.

"This is where they hide. The fishermen have no idea." He pets the fish's back. "Look at my little brother."

"Brother?"

"Well," he says. "Fine. My half brother. All of them. Half brothers and sisters."

"You have no idea which fish are the parents of which fish."

He brings his face down to the water and presses his cheek against the fish he's holding. "It doesn't matter. They're my siblings." Then he takes the seaweed he stole from me and feeds it to the fish, stroking its scales the whole time. The fish nibbles it up with the same teeth as Fishboy's. "There you go," Teeth says softly. "There."

If I didn't know better, I'd swear that fish was cuddling with him.

If I didn't want to believe that these fish are totally not sentient enough to worry about eating.

"They're not just any fish, you know?" Teeth gently lets the fish go. "I mean, eat the minnows. I eat the minnows. The minnows are stupid as fuck. They run into the rocks while they're swimming. The ancho . . . what are they?"

"Anchovies."

"Yeah. They're just assholes. Eat them if you want. Seriously, I'll even help you catch them. They taste okay."

"The fishermen catch those too, sometimes."

"Yeah, when one swims right into their net." He shakes his head. "They're hunting the Enkis. I know that. And I get that. But . . . we're special."

"The reason they want them is because they're special. Anchovies aren't going to cure anyone."

"That's not the special I mean." He catches another fish and hugs it to his chest.

I'm trying to be gentle. "They're only special to you because they're yours."

"I could say the same thing about that cute kid you were holding."

Well, shit.

I look away.

His voice is quiet. "It's not like I can have my own babies, you know? It's not like there are girls like me. Or anyones like me. And I don't even have the proper equipment. You know that. The fishermen sure as fuck do."

Now I look at him again. "The fishermen just rip at you."

And fuck, he lets them because he's dying to be touched. I know that because I know that feeling.

So I put my hand on his arm, of course I do, before I even register that he might not want that this second, but he fucking leans in to it, then shakes his head a little.

He says, "The fishermen just rip at me, but we're not talking about that right now." He holds up the fish in his hand as much as he can while still keeping it in the water. "You see him, this little thing, this trusting little thing? These guys are sort of . . . all I have."

This would probably be a good time to say, *You have a sister, and I made out with her.* But I can't tear myself away from that fish in his hands, its empty animal stare. It sees just as well as I do, but I don't want to think about that. But I am.

But then Teeth is looking at me with these swamp green eyes and going, "So it's time to stop eating my siblings, okay? Please. I'm saying please." He swallows. "Magic word and all that."

eleven

"JUST MAYBE WE CAN START WEANING HIM OFF, IS ALL I'M saying."

Mom picks up a cabbage and examines it. "Will you eat cabbage?"

"If you fry it in bacon."

She makes a face, but she puts it in her basket and pays anyway. I wonder what happens when we run out of money. We're going to have to find something to sell.

"Weaning him off, Mom."

"It feels too risky right now, Rudy. We're seeing so much improvement."

Mr. Gardener, the fat old man who lives closest to us,

bumbles past on his way to the homemade newspaper stand and shoves me stomach-first into the desk of the produce booth. I wince. Mr. Gardener ignores me and starts yelling at Mrs. Lauder, the produce lady, "I'm not paying fifty for that!" but he will, we all know he will, because every week he does. Eventually.

Sometimes it's like we're all playing these small parts in a play, and our job is to show up every Tuesday and say the same two lines, and go home.

My role is to scan the ocean for the fishboy until Fiona comes and handles me. I already see her watching me from her standard spot on the edge of the cliff. I think a strong wind could push her off. She winks at me. She always does.

I turn back to Mom. "So why would he go back to being sick once he's well?"

"The same reason we couldn't take him off medicine on good days. It's for maintenance."

"The medicine didn't work."

She laughs like she doesn't mean it. "That's pretty much the point, Rudy."

"Yeah, and now he's better than he's ever been."

"Exactly why we can't risk halting his progress now." She picks up one of the fish we bought with both hands and tips it back and forth, checking its weight. It's facing me, eyes round and smooth as marbles. I have to keep reminding myself that it's dead, and it can't see me.

I say, "I'm scared I'm becoming a vegetarian."

"You had three hamburgers yesterday."

"No, like, mentally becoming a vegetarian."

"And why's that such a bad thing?"

"Because vegetarians annoy me." I'm watching her put that fish into her tote bag, and I can't stop feeling like I'm going to throw up. I wish that one had swum away. I don't know.

Mom says, "You sound just like your father sometimes."

I wish I had a reason to think that it's more okay to eat them than it would be to carve up the fishermen and suck at the insides. I wish that was the cure Dylan needed.

No. I don't care about the fish, end of story. I haven't lost my knowledge that fish are fish, and whether or not they hug themselves against Teeth's slimy chest, they're fish. Teeth isn't interesting because he's half fish, but because he's half human. Or because he's just mine or whatever.

But . . . "But they're magic fish," I tell Mom. "Maybe they're more like . . . like mammals or something than we think. You know. Sentient. Maybe they're like dolphins."

"Oh, honey, don't say that."

"Just because we don't want to think it . . ."

It's so stupid. I would feed my brother dolphins if it would save him. I'd feed him babies if it would save him. Just . . . Dylan, okay?

It hits me for the first time that that might not be an okay thing to feel.

"We have no reason to believe that's true," she says.

"They're different from minnows and anchovies and stuff."

Mom says, "And minnows and anchovies don't save your brother's life."

I pick out apples. "I know." I've had this conversation before. Clearly I suck at arguing either side.

She squeezes a nectarine and lets it go. "He still has a long way to go, Rudy. Don't get me wrong, I'm so excited about all the progress he's made. But this isn't something to mess around with."

"So what's the endgame? It's not like there are schools here." There is no real life here.

"We'll go home someday," she says, but even she doesn't sound like she believes it anymore. How can she talk about going home in the same breath she admits the fish are tying us indefinitely here?

"Nobody ever goes home," I mumble.

She stops and hugs me. "Oh, sweetheart. Your brother loves you so much."

I have a headache.

She says, "Maybe someday there will be a good set of lungs for him at home, and we will look back on this as the thing that got him through the wait."

"I hope so." That does sound pretty perfect.

"Oh, look," Mom says. She lets me go. "Fresh fish."

The fishermen are hauling huge wicker baskets up to the stand, and now everyone in the marketplace is rushing over, haggling for a better price. But they'll pay anything. They're all in the same position as Dylan: saved from dying and petrified of being sick again. Without the fish, who knows if they'd go back to how they were: arthritic, diabetic, catatonic.

Of course no one ever leaves this island. No one's willing to risk it. Why would we ever be? We'd be too afraid that the lung transplant would fall through the way it did last year, and we wouldn't be able to get back here in time, and . . .

Ugh. I don't want to think about that shit. That fucking scrapbook, that fucking library, the fucking fishboy.

The fucking fact that staying here is starting to sound not so horrible.

God, I really was desperate for a friend.

But no, I think about leaving. I think about college. This is what I'm supposed to do. I taste that promise for as long as I can, rolling it around my tongue and letting it settle into my cheek. Until I leave them. Until I get on a plane or a boat and get so far away that no one can even see me. I am free. I am free.

I can get through a few years.

I won't get glued to this place.

I don't have to be.

I'll keep searching for exits all the time. Even when I don't want to.

I'm a horrible brother.

I'm still chewing on everything when Fiona comes over. "The ghost likes you," she whispers. She's leaning on my shoulder. She smells like she's from the ocean.

"You're crazy, Fiona."

"The ghost is with you," she rasps. "He isn't leaving anytime soon."

"He's not a ghost."

She smiles with her lips closed. "Who's *he?*"

"The . . ." I shake my head. "See you next week, Fiona."

One of the fishermen, the one missing an eye, looks over at me when my mom and I approach the booth. His hat is pulled low on his forehead. He grins at me with his gold teeth.

Why the hell *shouldn't* they be bastards, seriously? They rule us.

My mom hands over a fistful of bills and points to the fish she wants, and the fisherman starts wrapping them in paper. I'm focused, this time, on the money instead of the fish's dead eyes.

Fuck. We're paying them.

The guy I pulled off Teeth is slipping the money into his pocket right now. He's going to take it to Mr. Gardener's stand and buy cigarettes and some crackers and whatever the hell he wants.

I don't know why this hadn't occurred to me before.

We're eating Teeth's brothers and we're helping the guys who hurt him.

Mom makes me carry the fish home. I'm praying the whole walk by the water that Teeth doesn't see me with this bag. I don't see him, but I'm pretty sure that doesn't mean anything. He's maybe a better hider than we give him credit for.

God, if he sees me, I'm so fucked. He'll make me swim laps next lesson.

I say, "Can't we at least start catching the fish ourselves? Instead of buying them from the fishermen?" I know this wouldn't appease Teeth one bit, but it would make me feel better about the whole thing.

"They guard the bait with their lives, you know that."

"Power-hungry assholes."

"Sweetie, I wish it were simple too."

Mom thinks we should try to make amends with Ms. Delaney, so she asks me to bring over a bottle of wine from Dad's puny collection. I obviously decide to go over on a Tuesday evening. I'll let Diana give her the wine. Or maybe we can drink it.

Maybe I can get her drunk and get her to show me the diaries. God, I've never ended that sentence that way.

Diana peers through the curtains at me, then cracks the door open, grinning. "Good to see you." She's all dressed up again. She has her hair in a bun and glasses near the tip of her nose. I think she's going for sexy librarian. The glasses don't even have lenses. I'm smiling in spite of myself.

It's still temporary, but it's still amazing to feel something. Even when that something is just a tongue.

She pulls me inside, down the hallway, and backward onto her bed. I can't believe that after all this passion, manufactured though it may be, we haven't had sex yet. But I have to admit that the kissing is nice.

As is being half-drunk and crashed on her floor and talking about Kafka. I'm losing some kind of man card for this and I don't even care. Wine is nice.

"Did you finish *The Metamorphosis*?" she says.

I roll onto my stomach. "Yeah." She's fixing her hair. I like watching how quickly her fingers move.

"Well? I don't like it."

"Then why'd you give it to me?"

She grins. Her cheeks are getting all flushed. She gets more turned on when we talk about books than when we kiss. I shouldn't be okay with that. I'm beginning to think I'm using this girl as some kind of symbol and that's really not okay with me. I wish I were a different person. I kiss her like that will fix me.

"I loved it," I say. "It was the most relevant thing I've read in a long time."

"It doesn't make any sense."

"He's ostracized and they throw fruit at him and he dies. From loneliness."

She shakes her head. "The part where he turns into a bug."

"Or whatever."

"Or whatever. Why did that happen?"

"You don't know. That's the point. Sometimes there's just . . . a transformation. And there isn't a real explanation."

She considers this, winding the end of her braid around her finger. "I don't like that."

"Spoken like someone who lives her life in books."

She stretches like I've touched her. I wonder when I can ask about the diaries.

She says, "My father came by yesterday, and my mother threatened him with a gun."

Just when I've written her off, she can make one sentence more exciting than my entire life. I say, "Your mother has a gun?" I'm not sure my mother's even ever seen a gun in real life. I know I haven't.

"A silver handgun."

"Wow."

"She keeps it loaded."

"Um . . . damn."

"She is not a fan of my father. They were never in a real relationship and they still fight like married couples do in those books about teenagers. My mother thinks it was all a mistake. It was during a vulnerable time in her life. She is full of those, to be honest. My mother would not make a good heroine. She is weak and unsympathetic."

I guess that's how you talk about someone you know your whole life.

I guess that's kind of how you think about anyone when you're Diana.

I'm trying to figure out where Teeth fits into this. He's almost definitely older than Diana. But he's hard to age, with all the scales and that smile.

"He doesn't live on the island," Diana says. "He's one of the men who rides the shipping boat and unloads everything at the market. Usually he knows he's supposed to stay far away. I suppose he forgot."

I mentioned that boat to Fishboy the other day, and he lit all up like a little kid and said, "Oh, man, I *love* that boat. That boat is *so cool.*" To be honest, I think he's crazy about all boats, though he won't admit it, because of course fish aren't crazy about boats. But he knows a lot about them from all his time in the marina. He apparently listens well to what they're shouting back and forth when he's getting the shit beaten out of him. That's where he learned to curse, after all.

"Boats are the fucking kings of the universe," he'll say, his fin twitching like crazy as the ship pulls into the marina, and then he'll start babbling about the difference between port and starboard like this is supposed to be brand-new information for me. "I could totally be a . . . whatever."

"Sailor?"

"On a boat?"

"Yep."

"Yeah." He'll sigh all wistfully. "I could be a sailor. But I'm too busy being a fish."

Now Diana goes to her mirror over her dresser and puts on a bracelet. I've never seen a girl's room with less makeup. Even my mom has a lipstick or two on the nightstand. "Do your parents fight?" Diana says.

Softly, I say, "More than they used to."

"Maybe they're going to get divorced."

I didn't know you were allowed to just say that. I clear my throat. "Your mom still probably likes your father more than she likes your brother's father."

"This is your way of asking for the story." She sits down beside me. "The short and dark fable of my mother's ocean adventure."

I watch her. I don't say anything, If she really knew how much I want this, she would stop. She would keep teasing. It's not like she's the only one being used here.

I'm trying not to wonder why I care so much. It's curiosity. That's all it is. It doesn't have anything to do with how I feel about Teeth.

She says, "Four years before I was born, my mother decided to take a swim at almost exactly midnight. She's living all alone, because this is right after her parents died in a car accident, when they were on vacation in Capri. She's been told to never go into the ocean, that it isn't safe. And at this time, there are very few others living on the island. Fiona and her husband and some other people who are not at all important."

Yeah, it would be Fiona.

"So Mother wears her favorite bikini and goes down to the shore. A pink bikini. Her diary is very specific about the bikini. She usually used it for sunbathing. The diary implies there was once sun here. I don't know if that is for effect. Maybe this is like *Holes* and the weather is very metaphorical."

I have absolutely no options but to hear this story or to lie in bed at night and listen to the ocean and his screaming and wonder, wonder, imagine who is right. These are my only two choices.

I need to be right.

I need to hear that the fish are bad.

Diana lowers her voice to this dramatic whisper. "So she wades into the water, up to her hips. She's in too deep, it's too dark. She takes a step backward. She falls. She feels something pinch her skin, feels her bikini bottoms rip."

I'm picturing Fishboy doing this, even though I know that his part of the story doesn't come until later. I can't get the image out of my head, and it's scaring me.

With her voice so quiet I can hear the ocean groaning outside and the ticks of the clock on her shelf, each one so small and precise, like drops of water hitting the ground.

Diana says, "At first she thinks it's a piranha, but she looks down and sees a chubby Enki fish. Her father has told her horror stories about these fish. Their scales are poisonous, their teeth can crush rocks, they are only safe dead, but she's always been so fascinated, thought they were beautiful, loved them. Now she wonders if she can scoot out of the water before it bites her. And then . . ."

I stare. Her voice is so excited. I wonder if she forgot that this is something that really happened—to her mother—and not just some horror story she read in her library.

Diana says, "She looks down and sees the fish has entirely disappeared. And she feels so much pressure—"

"Wait—"

She nods. "The whole thing."

"No."

"The entire fish. En. Tire."

"Christ, Diana. That's disgusting."

She looks offended while she rolls onto her back and looks at me with her head tilted into the carpet. "It's not disgusting. Books are disgusting."

"I like books. I thought you liked books."

"Let's be honest, Rudy, books are pornography for brains.

All that subtext and bullshit and hidden imagery. This is real life. It isn't like that. Isn't that what you just said?"

"I . . ."

"You said, 'Sometimes there's just a transformation.'"

"I . . ."

"This is real life. This is a woman raped by a fish. And sometimes it just happens."

I've never hated getting what I want quite this much.

twelve

"YOUR FISH." DYLAN POINTS TOWARD THE SEA. "THERE?"

I see the tip of Teeth's tail poking out of the water. He does that on purpose when he knows I can't come be with him, just to screw with me. "Yep, there's one right there." If Teeth heard me tell my brother he's a fish, he'd never let me live it down. He'd do that little dance where he waves his arms around his head and go, "I'm a fish, I'm a fish!"

Sometimes, when I think about it too hard, I start wondering where Teeth learned how to be happy. I try not to think that hard, especially not about him.

To be honest, I'm having a hard time thinking about Teeth at all right now. I don't know. I don't know what to think. I've been avoiding the dock and spending more time at the mansion with Diana these past few days. I don't know if he really knows that. I really, really hope not.

I glance at Dad to make sure he hasn't noticed the fish tail that's a little too big to be real. But he's focused on the house, up by where Mom's cooking with the door open. We're sitting on the beach so close to the house that we can smell the fish she's frying. I can't see the dock from here, so I know Teeth came out of his way to wave his fin at me.

Dylan gets up by himself and scales the very edge of the shoreline, heel-toe, arms out for balance. He's right in front of our house, and I'm sure for a second that it's finally going to fall. And crush him. I watch his feet leaving tiny prints in the sand.

"What are you looking at?" Dad asks me.

I don't want to tell him. They get mushy when I admit I'm worried about Dyl. And I probably shouldn't admit my obsession with our house collapsing. He'd probably turn it into a metaphor. Something about my shit of a life. Enough metaphors.

I say, "Are you and Mom going to get divorced?" I don't know. Just to have something else to say. Just because I can't stop thinking about our house crumbling, and now I'm thinking about metaphors.

He double-takes like a cartoon character. "What?"

The ocean pounds three large waves in a row, like a drumbeat.

I say, "You never even talk anymore unless you're fighting."

"Hey, you're not around that much lately, kiddo." He wiggles his eyebrows a little when he says this.

I start talking fast, mostly so he doesn't get a chance to ask where I am all the time or why he apparently thinks I'm doing something eyebrow-wiggle worthy. I guess I'm glad they assume I'm spending all my time wooing Diana. I say, "It's just that ever since we've moved here it's like we became different people. And it's not like we've changed, or gotten better, or worse, it's just that . . . we stopped being who we really are and started being who we expected each other to be. We're like . . . caricatures, compared to how we were." I dig in the sand with my thumb. "It's like we're all trying to disappoint each other in exactly the same ways we always have, so that there are no surprises."

"Rudy."

"I'm all aloof and you and Mom are all . . . cramped."

"Cramped."

"In the tiny kitchen. And the house is so dark all the time. And the ocean's so loud. . . ."

He exhales. "This is a rough time. We know that."

"It's been a rough time for three years."

"But now you can't get away from it. And I understand how hard that must be for you. Leaving your friends . . ."

"It's not that." God, it has nothing to do with them.

How long has it had nothing to do with them?

Dad says, "But he's getting better now. Considerably." He looks down at Dylan and smiles. "Dyl, start heading back, okay?"

"Okay!" Dylan shouts. He turns around and starts coming toward us, still pretending he's on a balance beam.

I feel Teeth watching him.

"I know you don't like it here," Dad says.

"It's not that simple." I look back out to the water, but it's nearly still right now, and Teeth has disappeared.

"You miss home."

"Of course."

He says. "We're a family. And . . . unfortunately . . ." He puts an arm around my shoulders. "That means your mom and I are going to fight sometimes when things are this rough, and it also means no one's going to bail on anyone else. Even on you, kiddo."

I look at him.

He's giving me this encouraging smile that I don't deserve. "We know that you're not having an easy time here, and we're so sorry. And we haven't forgotten about you, you know?"

But the thing is that sometimes they have.

I feel my voice catching. "It's like you're mad at me all the time."

He doesn't take his eyes off me. It's like this was the part of the conversation he was waiting for, and he knows what I'm going to say before even I do. "Nobody's mad at you," he says. His voice is quiet, but it has all this air behind it.

"Like I don't love him as much as you guys do."

He frowns. "You feel like that?"

"No. You feel like that." I push my feet hard into the sand. I have this stupid thought that I want to get trapped where I'm sitting, just to prove to Dad that I'm not going to get up and run away. Then before that thought is even finished, my brain screams at me to get up and run away.

Dad's hand is suddenly on my shoulder, heavy and solid like a harness. He says, "It's normal to resent him. It doesn't make you bad. It's understandable. He gets a lot more attention than you do. And I'm sorry for that, Rudy. I really am. It's not as if, if we could . . . if we could have chosen things, this is where you would have ended up."

"It's not like that."

"You were our only kid for a long time." He gives me this little smile. "You were our whole world. We never would have planned for you to feel lost."

"That's not what I'm saying." Though I have to admit that something in there plucked me in a way I wish it hadn't. Because it sounds stupid to say that I'm my parents' second favorite. I'm too old, anyway, to give a shit whether or not Mommy and Daddy love me best. Give me a break.

It's stupid.

I tilt my head back and breathe out hard. Dylan is almost back to us. We need to finish this now. "I don't resent him," I say.

Dad watches me.

I choose my words as quickly as I can. "I am scared to death of him, Dad."

Dylan runs—runs—into me and crashes into my arms.

I say, "Hey, buddy," and give him a hug.

I think Dad is reaching out toward Dylan, but then he palms my head instead. And I can't tell which of us he's talking to when he says, "You make me so proud."

I don't want Dylan to see me cry again, so I hold my breath when he starts running around the beach in circles with his arms flailing around, looking exactly like this kid we've had in our heads for the past three years.

"Can I ask you a question?" Diana says, mid-kiss, not sexy, just conversational.

"Yeah."

"What's a swing set?"

"What?"

"They're in books, but no one ever explains what they are. They aren't in my encyclopedia."

"When I was a kid, someone told me that 'pear' wasn't in the dictionary and I never checked and I think about it *all the time.*"

"We can check later."

So I explain to her what a swing set is and then I try to tell her about TV and the Internet and all sorts of foreign crazy things and she rolls her eyes and reminds me how much you can learn from books and how much you really can't, like the feel of her waist in my hand, like sea air, like what a swing set is.

And her face when I tell her about Michigan, when I show her what to do once our pants are off . . . God, that fascinated face. I know that face.

My hand drifts to her hip and before I can stop it, before I can even process that I'm thinking it, my brain thinks, *What would it feel like to touch scales, tail, scars?* and I'm kissing her deeper without meaning to and okay, fine, it's fine, who the fuck *hasn't* had a mermaid fantasy? That's something you can get from a book. That's something that's not real. It's fine.

No, what's actually weird is that I'm not really that concerned.

"Where have you been, kiddo?" Fishboy says as I make my way down the dock afterward. "Christ. No, I know where you've been. Don't answer that."

"Hmm?" I sit down and plunk my feet in the water. It hurts in a good way. "I need to talk to you."

"I don't want to talk."

"It's about the fish."

"What about my fish?"

"Have you ever seen them hurt anyone? Anybody?"

"Like a human?"

"Yeah."

He frowns. "Of course not. You know what I have seen? Humans hurting fish."

"It's not the same. No. Stop. You can't say it's the same. I . . . I don't know, Teeth."

It's not as if people are going out and capturing his fish just to do it. We catch them because we need them to live. What did the fish get out of impregnating Ms. Delaney? What good did that do them?

I look at Teeth, bobbing in the water.

Shit.

Teeth frowns at me. "What?"

They needed something to keep them alive too.

I have to stay still for a few minutes just to collect everything in me. I can't believe I'm weighing the morality of hurting a fish versus hurting a human. But it's so hard not to compare the two with that creature in the water in front of me, sucking on his fingers.

"What are you *thinking* about?" he says.

"What would you say if I told you a fish hurt someone? Really hurt them?"

He's making eye contact so fierce it scares me. "I'd say the fishermen hurt me every night."

"Hurt you—"

"No. *Really* hurt me."

"I—"

"Fuck humans! I hate humans. What the fuck do you want from me? I don't give a shit about your little human stories, okay? Some fish are bad, and do you have any idea how many humans have fucked me over? Goddamn it, Rudy!"

I try to say something, I don't even know what, but then he dives under the water and he's gone.

thirteen

AND THE NEXT DAY, IT'S LIKE IT NEVER HAPPENED.

"So I know where you came from, by the way," I say.

"Humans and a house and all that. Yeah, I know." Fishboy isn't even looking at me. His eyes are busy tracking something under the water.

"That house. The big one, right there."

"You must think I'm an idiot."

"What are you looking at?"

"I'm—" He dives and emerges with a tiny fish in his mouth. He spits it onto the deck. "Look at that! Check that out! Oh, man, Teeth is the king. Teeth is the king. I am the king of the seas. Look at that."

I squirm away from it. It's flopping around like my brother during a bad night. "What is it?"

"Minnow. Oh, God, look at this minnow. Mmm. It's beautiful." He kisses it and cuddles it against his cheek, then neatly slits its head off with his teeth.

"Oh, Jesus, Fishboy."

He looks up, a laugh, halfway through, frozen on his face. "What did you call me?"

"Fishboy." But I didn't mean to. Shit. "It's, uh, what I called you in my head before I knew your name."

He shrugs and nods a little. "Fishboy. Yeah, that's cool."

Thank God. This would have been such a stupid fucking thing to fight about.

He's really grossing me out with this fish, licking the blood off its neck, so I shake my head quickly and say, "You know how I found out where you're from?"

"I don't care."

"I made out with your sister."

"What's 'made out'?" He's looking at me with these huge eyes.

"Kissed."

"Ew," he says. "You kissed a fish?" Then he buries his face in the minnow and rips it to pieces.

"This is so gross."

He comes up with flesh speared on his teeth. "Oh my

God. Rudy, this is the best minnow in the world. You have to try this."

"I'll pass."

"I'll save you the *liiiiver.*"

At least now I know he's screwing with me. "Do fish even have livers?"

"You're a liver."

"How do you know that word?"

"I'm very, very smart." He licks the skin clean. "Oh my God. Minnow. You are a beautiful minnow."

"It's dead."

"It doesn't speak English anyway. Oh, lovely, lovely minnow."

"You're disgusting."

"You're the one kissing a fish. Gross."

"Your human sister."

"I knew what you meant. Seriously. You think I'm an idiot, don't you?"

I smile and he smiles and I lie down on my back, as far as I can get from the remains of the fishboy's lunch. He's sucking on all the little bones.

Eventually he finishes eating, and I don't say anything, and he doesn't say anything. He reaches up to the dock and walks the fish bones back and forth like they're people. I half-watch his hands and half-watch the sky. It's the first time we've been absolutely silent together when it doesn't feel like we're fighting. It almost feels like we're tucked in to go to sleep. The silence must last nearly five minutes before he looks up at me and smiles.

It doesn't matter what team I'm on, for a minute. For a minute it's just me and that smile.

"If you're done relaying my family history to me," he says, "I have a mission for us."

I sit up. All the blood rushes out of my head and makes me dizzy.

"I knew that would make you pay attention. Poor, bored Rudy."

"What are we doing?"

"Operation Enki Freedom."

"Seriously, how do you even know these words?"

"Ms. Klesko listens to the radio without her hearing whatevers in. And I am very, very smart, Rudy. You're in?"

I guess freeing a few can't hurt. The fact is, my mom brought a whole school of fish home from the market this week, and the guilt is eating me alive.

"Come ooooon," Teeth whines. "Operation Save My Brothers."

Now it's not like I have a choice. "Yeah, I'm in."

Fishboy licks his lips. "Excellent. Come on. Let's go swimming!"

I slip into the water. I start shivering from the second my

toe breaks the surface. At least I'm more confident in the water now, after all the swimming lessons. Thank God Mom and Dad think I'm fucking Diana, or I'd have no excuse for why I'm gone so much.

We swim. I let him lead, and I grab on to his tail when I get a little shaky in the deep water. He lets me, but not for too long, since it makes him a lot slower.

He doesn't swim like I do; he taught me how to flutter kick, but he hits the water with huge strokes of his tail, like an oar on a rowboat. He can hold his breath for almost three minutes. I timed him once. He says that with practice, I can stay underwater for that long too. I want to learn.

We're heading toward the marina again. Shit. I hope this isn't a suicide mission. He should have disclosed that before he dragged me along. I still might have come.

He stops us against a cluster of algae-coated rocks. They're slippery, and I can't get a good grip, so I latch on to his arm. He doesn't shake me off.

"What are you looking at?" I say.

"Fishermen."

My fingers tighten on his arm. "Teeth, come on. Let's get out of here. I've seen the fish. Hi, fish." I see them now, swirling around his tail. He's leaning in to them when he can.

"Seen these?" He pulls me around the corner and shows me an enormous net filled with fish, hauled halfway out of the water. The fish struggle all together, like one huge animal.

There must be a thousand of them. I can't believe we eat that much fish, as an island. But even my tiny brother can go through four or five a day, I guess. And I can think of ten people off the top of my head who don't eat a thing but fish.

The fishboy grits his teeth. "Look at that. Look at what they're doing. And they don't even have the common decency to kill them quickly. They're going to let them flop around in the sun until they drown."

"'Drown' means water."

"Whatever."

"If the fishermen catch you, I don't think they'll have the decency to kill you quickly, either."

"Well, that's the truth."

I pull his wrist. "Why are you being stupid?"

He glares at me. "I'm stronger than the fucking fishermen. Plus they're at lunch."

"They're twice your size."

"Then why do I always get away?" He looks at me like my brother does when he gives me his stupid five-year-old comebacks. *I know you are, but what am I?* "How come they can't capture me for more than an hour?"

I don't have an answer for that, so he crosses his arms, triumphant, which throws my hand off his arm and leaves me treading water on my own.

He says, "I can't gnaw through that rope. If I could, the fish could too, and the fishermen aren't that stupid. The rope is too strong. My teeth just bend against it."

"Ow."

"Yeah."

"So how are we doing this?"

"Well, see, *I can*, however, slit through the individual whatevers of each rope if I turn my head the right way. The fishermen are *that* stupid."

"The fibers?"

"Fiber's that thing you eat, Rudy. I'm talking biting through."

I shake my head. "You've done this before?"

"Once." He licks his lips. "A year ago."

"It worked?"

"They caught me before I could make much of a hole in the net." His eyes get a funny glaze. Remembering. One of his hands travels to the back of his tail, right over where his tailbone is, or would be, I don't know.

I swallow. "This is a bad idea."

"Anyway, that time I didn't have a lookout. Now I have a lookout." He plants his hand on my shoulder and looks at me seriously. "This is a very, very easy job, Rudy. You hold on to the dock and you keep out of sight, but you do some kind of whatever if you see a fisherman coming."

"Okay, some kind of what?"

"God, I have to tell you everything." He whistles. "Like that."

"Got it. That one was hard to figure out from context, sorry."

"What the fuck is context?"

I laugh. "Never mind."

"You're so annoying."

"Are we doing this?"

At home it was always me coming up with the crazy plans and forcing my friends to follow. Maybe that's why I'm into this—following along, I mean. It gives me the chance to pretend I'm someone else.

My hand is on his arm again. I really am easy.

"So we're going to do this on my count," he says.

"Okay."

"Except, see, I like to concentrate when I'm counting, and right now I'm busy keeping watch. So."

I look at him. "So we're doing this on my count?"

"Yeah."

"When I say three?"

"Three. All right."

"It's going to come after two."

"I know numbers, Rudy." But after a beat he says, "Two. Okay. So that's when I'll get ready."

Or maybe it's conversations like these that are the reason I'll do crazy shit with the fishboy. Because I haven't felt like this in a really long time. It's hard to explain. Like I said, I'm easy.

"One. Two."

He gets all twitchy, flexing his fingers and getting ready to push off the rocks. I'm trying not to laugh.

"Three!"

He grabs my hand and we jet forward. He's swimming so fast that bubbles rush to the surface with each stroke of his tail. We swim into the marina, and he gets me settled on the dock, then he grabs the net and starts slicing away with those sword teeth. I turn the other way and lower myself between the bottom of the dock and the surface of the water. I feel like an alligator. This is how I find Teeth all the time, floating on his back underneath the dock where no one can see him. Now I need to pray that no one can see me, either.

No sign of the fishermen. Just when I'm about to ask Teeth how it's going, I hear the *swish-plop* behind me of a fish hitting the water.

"He's swimming!" Teeth whispers. "He's alive!"

It's hard to think about the implications of freeing maybe-violent fish when I hear how happy Teeth is. So I just say, "No fishermen so far."

"Good. Careful. They're sneaky." I hear a few more rips of his teeth, and I can't help but turn around when he cheers and starts laughing. As soon as I turn my head, the

the fish start pouring out like a rainfall. I catch glimpses of Teeth through the downpour of scales. He's grinning like a maniac and dancing among the fish. "Safe! Safe safe safe babies!"

"Okay," I say. "Now we get the fuck out of here."

"Right. Out of here!" And then he takes off. He leaves me. Shit.

I can't believe this. He's leaving me with the fishermen. Christ. He set me up. Fuck.

He is a fish after all.

He left them a new boy and now he's swimming away and fuck, why the fuck did I trust him? Am I fucking crazy? Who the fuck trusts a fish?

I could be with Diana right now.

Shit. This is just the kind of crap you fall into when you live on an island for too long. I wanted a friend so badly that I latched on to the first guy who smiled at me.

I am way, way too easy.

Never again. Never fucking ever again. If I get out of here, I'm never getting screwed over again. I'll stick with girls who stay inside, if that's what it takes. I don't need this shit. I need drunk girls in trash bags and friends who step on my brother's breathing machine. I don't need these fucking feelings.

I can't believe he did this.

Okay. This is going to be fine. The water's deep, but if I

can just push off the dock, if I don't get disoriented, if the fishermen don't catch me, shit, shit—

But then he's back.

Oh.

He laughs and grabs me. "Sorry!" Oh my God. He's *hugging* me. He says, "Thought you were behind me. I'm sorry! You're such a shitty swimmer!"

And then he's throwing me into the water and pulling me along with him, and we're out of there.

And fuck it, because that was seriously fucking fantastic.

Once we're back to safety, we float on our backs by the sandbar. Teeth does big, lazy kicks.

I'm so tired. If the water weren't just a few feet deep, I'd probably be freaking out that I might fall asleep and drown, and Teeth would forget about me again, even if it's just for a minute. Though I once read something that said babies can drown in like four inches of water. I wonder how many inches it would take with me. He better not forget about me again.

Teeth is singing about wanting another minnow. He cannot carry a tune at all.

Mostly just to make him for the love of God shut up, I say, "So I am seriously almost sleeping with your sister."

"Why do you keep talking about that?"

Because I like it. Because I'm waiting for you to care. "I thought you'd be interested."

"This isn't, like, my life. I don't care. I hate humans." Then he doesn't talk for a minute. I stroke behind me, my arms moving in circles.

"How old is she?" he says.

"Your sister?"

"Yes."

"About my age."

"Oh. How old are you?"

"Sixteen."

"I'm not sure how old I am."

I know Diana told me how long the fish-bikini thing was before she was born, but I can't remember how many years she said. So I say, "Probably nineteen or twenty. Older than me."

"Yeah. Older than the baby."

"I wonder how long fishboys live."

"Forever."

I say, "Wait. What baby?"

"My sister."

"Not a baby, you know?"

"I know that. I see her sometimes. She just . . . was. Fussy baby."

"You knew her?"

"Yeah, so I knew her when she was a baby. I didn't know her. She was a baby. Like, whatever. Stupid baby. Didn't have a personality."

"So you were still in the mansion when she was born."

He sits up in the water, so I do too. I can only see his torso. He looks like a regular boy with a bad skin condition. I have a hard time staying afloat this way, but I want to be able to watch him.

He isn't looking at me, just splashing the water with his hands and watching the ripples. "What did she tell you about me?" He barely moves his lips when he talks.

"Nothing," I say, which is sort of true. I want those fucking diaries.

He lived in that house. For years.

Teeth clears his throat. "I don't care about her. She's a human."

"You're half-human."

He mumbles something about me being half-asshole.

I say, "What makes fish better than humans, huh?"

"Better tails."

"Fishboy."

"Humans suck."

"What about the minnows?"

"Minnows are delicious."

"And they're fish. Like you or whatever."

He plays with his tail. "The minnows have their own brothers to worry about them."

I'm quiet. Teeth gives me a minute, because he knows what I'm thinking about.

I say, "You know, fish aren't perfect." I can't believe these are sentences in my life. "Your mom . . ."

He shakes his head. He doesn't like the word "mom," I can tell.

"The fishermen," he says softly. "Did you not get how this conversation really sucked the first time? Do we have to?"

"Hey. We don't. You okay?"

"I'm bored of this. I want to hear about you. Favorite color. Go."

I laugh. "Green."

"I'm green!"

"Fuck yeah you are."

"Why are you laughing? Isn't this what friends do?"

"Interrogate each other?"

"What? Uh, sure. I don't know what that means. But yes."

I lean my head back as far as it will go, letting the water creep over my head and onto my forehead. "See, I know what having friends is like, because they are something that I had. Have you . . . ever had a friend?"

This horrible question doesn't seem to make him sad. "Fiona used to feed me."

"Really?" So she does know. I knew it. She's talking in weird fortune-teller code. Someday, years from now, when something, anything, has happened that will make sharing the fishboy with someone okay, I'll rub Mom's face in the fact that Fiona isn't crazy. Just a little handsy.

Teeth says, "Yeah, when I was . . . after . . ." He's either confused or upset and doing a good job of hiding it. "I mean, before I was big enough to catch anything, and I was just floating around and crying and stuff . . . she would give me bread and carrots and stuff in the morning. Healthy shit. She was really into that. She's still alive, right?"

"Yeah."

"I haven't seen her in forever."

"She stands by the cliffs on Tuesday mornings, at the marketplace. Always. I . . . think she looks for you."

"I can't go over there. Too many people."

That might be the first time I've heard him say "people" instead of "humans." "What are you afraid of?"

He shakes his head. "If you see Fiona, say thanks? I never said thanks."

"Oh. Sure."

"Your friends. I want to hear about your friends."

I paddle myself in circles. "They're not even really my friends anymore. They were . . . before we moved here. Forever ago."

"Like a hundred days ago."

"Yeah?"

"I'm good with days. Sunrises."

I don't think I've ever seen him sleep. "A minute ago you couldn't count to three."

"Could too. Was making you feel smart. I'm a great friend."

"It feels like we've been here forever." I hold my breath and sink under the water for a minute. "And I haven't heard from them since I left."

"You miss them?"

"I guess. They were fun, you know?" The sun is setting now. I should be colder than I am. I close my eyes. "It's not like I really needed them or anything. They just made stuff more fun."

"I gotta be honest, you sound like a shitty friend right now."

"Hey." I start to sit up again, but it unbalances me and I start to sink, this time involuntarily. The water is a lot deeper than I thought. I start kicking hard to roll myself over, and then I feel Fishboy's arms scoop me up and toss me onto the sandbank.

"Don't do that," he says.

I breathe hard. "Thanks."

"Why didn't they move with you?"

I catch my breath. "What?"

"Your friends."

"It . . . doesn't work like that. They couldn't leave home just because I did."

"Why not? If you moved without me, I'd be pissed."

I look at him and wonder how the fuck exactly he thinks

he could follow me anywhere farther than the dock. My stomach hurts a little. I don't know how to tell him that friends at home weren't anything like this, because then I'm scared he'll ask what this is. And . . . God.

I shake my head a little and say, "They have stuff at home that's more important than I am. They have families and school and, like, reasons to stay."

"They have fish."

"Yeah, there's fish . . ."

"No, I mean . . . stuff to take care of."

"Well, yeah. Metaphorical fish."

He doesn't even pause to try to understand that word. "Fish who need them. And your fish came here, so you came here too."

"Yeah."

He kicks his fin. "I wish we could get away from our fish."

I feel like I just breathed in some water, but I don't think I did. I think it's just how my throat feels right now. "You do?"

"Yeah. Everything would be a lot easier if you could just dump fish the way humans dump their families."

"No, wait. I'm talking about . . . you realize me and my friends don't *actually* have fish, right? I should probably have told you what metaphorical means. My family is my fish."

"I hate being responsible. I mean, I like the idea of being

responsible. Like that fox, the one in that story? And he's in love with that other fox, and the bear sings a song . . ."

"What?"

"You know what I mean. Um . . . there's a tiger. He's bad. He's a king."

"Oh, shit." My brother loves this movie. "Robin Hood?"

"Robin Hood. Yes."

My throat hurts again, God fucking damn it.

He says, "I like the idea of being fish Robin Hood."

"You just made a metaphor. God, you're something."

"But I wish I could just . . . go. You know. Leave."

"So why don't you?"

His voice is quiet. "They need me. The fish and . . ." He gestures toward the marina. "And yeah. I don't even know what to be if they don't need me. I wish I could have different fish. Exchange them for new, exciting fish. With different fishermen."

After a while he breathes out. "Okay, so once upon a time, there was this boy who didn't have any legs. Like, no legs, okay? And he had some weird skin, and his Mom hid him away and kept him and whatevered him and she carried him everywhere and read him a lot of stories and cried and prayed. And his mom fed him fish again and again, but he never got better no matter what she did and she didn't know why. And the boy never even went outside, not once. This half a boy with no legs, you know?"

I nod.

"No one even knew that he existed because his mom barely left either. People came by with food and stuff, but the boy had to hide in his room whenever anyone came. His mom would put him in his room and close the door. His room had lots of books and toys and he could kind of drag himself around with his arms . . . and then Mom would come and she'd say, *I love you, I'll do whatever you need, I'll keep you safe.*"

I sit on the sandbar and watch him. He isn't looking at me.

He says, "But besides the skin and the no feet and staying inside, he was a pretty normal kid, and he breathed air like Mom, and he loved her and she loved him. Or you know, the love thing, whatever it is. They said *I love you* all the time. And he didn't care about being half, because he was happy."

I feel the same way I did in Diana's room. Exactly the same. When I knew she was going to tell me something horrible.

Teeth looks at me and says, "And she taught him lots of *words*."

I swallow. "Okay."

"So I know words."

"Yeah."

He curls his tail underneath himself. "And every night she'd tuck me in and she'd say, *grow feet grow legs grow legs,* because she wanted me to be big and tall and real and walking."

I want to say, *You're real,* but it would sound so stupid. He knows that. He's known that a lot longer than I've known that.

God, they call him a ghost.

"And then one day, surprise, boy is four years old, Mom's about to have a new baby, talking to the boy all the time about his new sister and how he's going to be so happy, and she's going to be big and strong with legs. She's going to be a real kid instead of half a kid. And Mom has the baby and she loves her, she loves the baby. The whole baby."

"Oh . . ."

"And that's when the half boy starts growing fins. Well. One fin." He looks at himself. "A tail and a fin. A really big fin. The tail's kind of titchy. I like my fin."

"Yeah."

"And then he gets webs between his fingers and scales all over his chest, and his teeth grow long and skinny and more and more of them, and he gets cold and slimy and . . ."

"Yeah. It's okay." *You can stop. Please stop.*

"And this woman, she could handle half a baby, she could hug that and put it to bed and cry about it, but she can't handle half a baby and half a fish, because she hated fish, and she just wanted to eat fish all the time and kill all the fish, and after the boy . . . after the fishboy got his tail she didn't even look at him ever again and she says she doesn't know what to do and she throws him into the ocean and loves her new baby and eats more fish than any person ever should." He digs into the sandbar.

I don't know what to say.

She threw him in.

"And Fiona fed me until I grew up." He shrugs. "I didn't want her to feed me. I don't want humans to feed me."

She threw him away.

"You could go back, you know? Or you could come stay at my house or something." I actually don't know how that last one would work. I can't picture my parents believing in Teeth any more than I could picture them dealing with a sick kid before we had to.

But they would never throw Dylan away. And it's not like he's the son they wanted.

And knowing this is the only thing keeping me from screaming *I hate humans*.

"Your parents would be scared of me," he says.

"They'd deal."

"They'd think I'm ugly."

"Teeth."

"I'd steal all their fish and throw them back in the ocean."

"They're already dead when we get them," I say, but it's enough for me to understand that having Teeth in the house would probably drive us all insane. It's not like I was seriously considering it, anyway. I knew he wouldn't do it.

The look on his face, though, says that maybe he would. But he shakes his head quickly. "It doesn't even make sense. How would I get up there?" He clears his throat. "Did you miss the part where I don't have legs? It is kind of important. God, you never listen to me." He flops backward into the water. He's breathing kind of hard. I'm watching his ribs.

"You could crawl," I say.

"The sun hurts my scales." He's yelling because his ears are full of water. I yank him so he's sitting up again. He frowns at me.

"Yeah, you'll see how you're frowning when someone starts to wonder what the fuck a boy is doing yelling about his scales."

"I'm a ghost, remember? Wooooo. I could yell about anything. *I eat your babies!*"

"I could help you get on land. Carry you or something."

"Big strong Rudy," he quips. "Look. I don't want to go on land. I hate humans."

"What about me?"

He kicks his fin.

"You know, that thing about how all fish aren't like the one that hurt your mom? We're not all like the fishermen either. Or like your mom."

"That lady."

"Yeah." I sigh. "If I were you, I'd just get the fuck out of here. Since you don't want to be around any of us. I don't know why you stay. Just to stare at the Delaneys?" I wonder what his name was when he was a boy.

"I can't stare at them. They never come outside."

"Your sister does sometimes."

"Whatever."

"There's nothing for you here."

"The fish."

I want to argue with this. I so, so do. I want nothing more in the whole world than to know how to argue why it's okay for Teeth to leave his family.

But I don't know how.

After a minute he says, "It's not just that. I can't just swim away."

"Why not?"

"I'm afraid I'll drown." He looks up and gives the world's smallest smile. He takes a deep breath with those lungs. "I'm afraid I'll drown."

I can't sleep. He's screaming like nothing I've ever heard. I wish the ocean were louder. I shouldn't have let him free the fish. Did I think the fishermen wouldn't find out, wouldn't know he was behind it? I shouldn't have helped. He wouldn't have done it alone.

I should have stayed with him tonight.

My room shakes in the wind, but even though my dresser and my mirror are rattling, I still hear the screaming. I wish the house would finally crumble into the sea, just to make noise, just because it's going to happen someday anyway, just to be something else to think about. I wish we would all just fall apart so I wouldn't have to listen to the downfall happen, so slowly, so painfully. Clawing at us.

fourteen

THAT TUESDAY, MARKETPLACE DAY, I STAYED UP HALF THE NIGHT listening to him scream and I'm nodding off into my oatmeal when my mom comes home from the market with one solitary fish.

I guess I'm just stupid, but the ramifications of what Teeth and I did doesn't hit me until just then, when she's standing at the door, staring at this puny fish, her face smushed into a ball.

Oh my God.

Fuck.

"What happened?" Dad asks. He's standing up, the dish towel draped over his shoulder, and coming to the door to hold her together. "Did you get there too late? We'll just have to ask someone for a few extra."

No. There aren't extra.

Fuck. I feel like I just ate something alive with my breakfast. I think Mom's going to cry, which is one of the signs of the end of my world.

She isn't steel. "They had such a small batch today. Everyone got one."

And then she's crying.

Shit.

I stand up. "I'm going to run to the marketplace," I tell her. "I'll barter fish off someone."

"Rudy, I don't know if . . ." She doesn't know how to finish this sentence.

"Maybe the fishermen will come in with a new load."

She nods and shoves a bunch of money into my hand, then grabs me into a tight hug. Every second she holds on makes me feel sore and sick.

"I've got to go," I say, and I pull out of the hug and sprint toward the marketplace. I think I hear Teeth calling me, but I won't look over. No fucking way. I can't.

I didn't think.

I didn't even think about Dylan.

Oh my God. I have to stop running because my stomach hurts too much. I bend over and wrap my arms around my waist while I catch my breath. I shouldn't have stopped, because now everything is hitting me a hundred times harder.

I sacrificed my brother to be wild for an afternoon.

I killed him so I wouldn't be lonely.

No. This isn't over yet. This is exactly like when I was clinging to the dock in the marina, and I thought my life was over. There is always an escape route. There's always a way. And there's always someone who's going to appear and save the day.

Maybe today it's me.

But when I get to the marketplace, all I see are twenty people wearing the same expressions as mine. All the wares are packed up, and they're just standing with fistfuls of money, craning their necks toward the marina, waiting for fish.

Sam is shaking when he turns to me and says, "If my wife doesn't get fish this week . . ."

"My brother."

"Me," Mrs. Lewis says.

I look at all of them, look at their fists. Then I count the money in my hand. They have so much more than I do. Even if the fishermen do bring a load in this late, I am not going to be able to compete with these people.

And the fishermen aren't coming.

There's a hand on my shoulder. Either it's shaking or I am. I turn and face Fiona. Okay, so definitely me, then.

"Your ghost is screaming," she tells me.

I can't take this. I start to go, and then I turn around, because I can't leave her yet, because I made a promise to the fishboy. And because if I don't keep it, it will stick in my head, and I cannot think about Teeth right now. I can't. I need to do this for him and get rid of it so he cannot exist.

So I say, as quietly as I can, "Thank you for taking care of him. I told him I'd tell you."

She looks at me for a long time. Her eyes are the palest blue I've ever seen.

"Thank *you*," she says.

So in the end, keeping the promise didn't help, because I'm walking home thinking about who I should have taken care of, and I'm throwing up on the beach.

It happens slowly.

First, he stops running. Then he's raising his arms up in the air every time someone passes him, silently asking to be carried. Then, when we're giving the smallest meals with the smallest bits of fish, he's coughing until he throws it all up.

We take turns pounding shit out of his chest and it barely makes a dent. I stop leaving the house. I know that out there everyone's trying to figure out bait, everyone's threatening the fishermen, everyone's trying a hundred ways, but it's fucking useless and no one knows it more than me. Almost every thought in my head is *run*, but it just stops being an option. I might as well be thinking *fly*. I can't do it. I can barely even go to the empty market every day when Mom sends me, just to check if maybe, maybe there are fish. There never are, because I guess fucking Teeth was encouraged by our success, I don't know, and every second I'm out of the house burns in my chest. I definitely don't look at the water when I go, but a few times I've heard the fishboy calling my name. Quietly.

But what the fuck is there to say to him? That I'm mad, but not as mad as I should be? That I don't really think fish are more valuable than people, but that's essentially the choice I made? That I made it because I wanted him to like me? Please stop? I thought you needed me?

I am the worst brother in existence, and it's not even because of the things I do and know are terrible. It's the stuff I don't notice, because he isn't on my mind.

I should never have made a mistake like that.

I don't know. I can't think about this anymore.

We watch TV in the evenings now, just to avoid talking to each other. Mom and Dad haven't fought once since the fish ran out, or if they do, it's whisper-fights in their room, and they come out looking close to stone. Mom had the breakdown initially, but since then I haven't seen a feeling from either one of them.

It's not that I think the emotions aren't there, I just wish that they'd show them so I could show mine. Because I can't be the one who's not strong enough for Dylan right now. I can't do it. I need to be the strongest one. Because the kid has no idea what's going on, and every strangled breath he takes is completely terrifying him, and . . . shit.

He trusts us.

We're all just quiet. It's like we're afraid if we talk, we'll miss someone opening their mouth and coming up with the solution to everything. So we sit and stare and wait for someone else to come up with the answer.

When I go into town, when Mom makes me, it's more of the same, and the guilt blooms in my stomach. Sam's wife hasn't been out of bed in days, and you can see the tumor in Leann's neck growing back and pressing against her skin. Mrs. Lewis collapsed on the beach a few days ago. Nobody's died yet, but it's just a matter of time, and I have to get home. I can't stand this.

I really didn't think we were this reliant. I really didn't.

And they're grabbing Teeth harder and he's crying louder every night and I lost my only friend, so in what way wasn't this a hideous mistake?

I'm a shaky mess all the time.

My parents have no idea this is all my fault, that they should be tying me down and excising me or lancing me like a boil or shooting me full of poison, anything, and then taking my lungs and stuffing them down my brother's throat and watching him turn pink again.

I have a dream about carving Teeth open and taking

his liver and giving it to Dylan, and Dylan keeps asking me what a liver is.

But I can't even fool myself into thinking my parents would want me dead, because I see how badly they need me right now, how they need me to be the one who leaves the house for milk and no fish, because they couldn't stand it right now. They need me because I'm the only one who can leave Dylan, even for a second.

"It's not going to happen," I growl at him when he's asleep. "So stop even thinking about it."

Mom holds him and strokes his hair and he asks—sometimes with words, when he can, sometimes just with his eyes—what the hell is going on, why the fuck he feels so sick. "Only a bump in the road," she says to him.

I wonder what the fuck road she thinks we're on. There aren't even any cars on this island.

I trap Dylan on my lap with my arms and listen to him wheeze. We put together puzzles. When he's falling back asleep, I whisper, "Breathe breathe breathe breathe," over and over again, my forehead up against his.

I don't care how much time he has left; he needs to be spending every second of it listening to every single thing I'm telling him right now. Because I am telling him some important shit.

"Don't you fucking dare," I whisper.

On our doorstep there is half a fish, the head and half a body. It's wrapped in wax paper. It's cool enough out here that it's like it's been refrigerated, but really it doesn't matter how long it's been waiting for us. Magic fish don't spoil.

The footprints in the sand are small, and the note says:

Mom's sick, could spare this, hope it helps. —D.

My parents act all grateful, like they don't know that half a fish isn't going to do shit.

Dylan is worse today, but something inside me has let go a little, and when Mom tells me to go down to the marina again to check for more fish, I go. I've gone a few times most days, just to beg for something. But they've been holding on to what they've caught this week very tightly, selling it to the rich old women on the island whose hearts haven't been beating right since the shortage at the market. Even though Dad tells me to spend whatever I have to get my hands on a fish, one single fucking fish, they're always already reserved for someone else who's paid even more. I can't believe this. It's like nobody in the world cares about a dying kid anymore. Except Diana, and even she didn't care enough to matter.

If I steal one, they'll never give my family another fish

again, but I don't know how long that will be a problem for us.

"Rudy."

I look over and there he is, bobbing in the water. He looks worse than I've ever seen him. He has bruises and scabs all across one cheek. I knew by the screams that the fishermen were really punishing him, but I didn't know he'd look this bad. It's more bruising than I've ever seen, and he's wearing this expression like he doesn't even notice. And it makes it very hard for me to be as mad at him as I want to be. My anger's more a thought than a feeling. Maybe I don't have room for any more feelings right now.

Except no, because apparently I still have room for my throat to tighten when I'm around him. Goddamn it, Rudy.

I pull my jacket around myself. "It's cold."

"Where have you been all week?"

"My brother's sick." I say this with as much meaning as I can. I punch out each word like I'm trying to hit him with it. I don't know if I can make this statement weigh as much as it really does.

But he looks down. He gets it. And now he doesn't know what to say. I see all the possible sentences flashing across his face.

He eventually settles on, "Is he okay?"

God. "No. He was up all night puking and he can't take a single step. He's fucked. I can't even believe we . . ."

I put my hand against my forehead and rub as hard as I can.

I can't even believe we.

"But it's not that many," Fishboy says, his voice all desperate. "The fishermen will catch a ton more and bring them to market—"

"Teeth, I'm not a fucking idiot. You're still slitting nets."

"A few, okay, maybe, but they're the ones who bring me to the mar—"

"Teeth, this isn't a fucking game, okay?" I charge toward the water, but I don't let it hit my shoes. "This isn't fucking Operation Anything besides Operation Watch Your Brother Die and it fucking sucks!"

He pushes his chest out. "You think I don't know that? You think *I of all*—"

"Fuck you." I leave him and walk the rest of the way to the marina.

"You didn't do it for the fish, you did it for me!" he screams, but I can't tell if he's trying to comfort me or condemn me. I don't know what he means. I don't know why I try to listen to him.

Hanging out with the fishboy has been a horrible life decision. I'm lying to my parents and sneaking out, I'm not spending nearly as much time with Diana as I should be, even if the time I spend with her is time I'd rather be spending with him, but I shouldn't be spending time with him, because it doesn't make any sense why I want to be with him, and I shouldn't . . .

Too many feelings.

If he calls my name one more time, I swear to God I'm going to hit him, and I don't know if I'll let him go like the fishermen do. I don't know if I could.

Except with every exhale, all this anger is leaving me, because there's really no point in blaming this all on him. I'm not fooling myself, and it isn't making me feel any better. I was the lookout. I'm as much to blame as he is.

God. Shit.

I ignore the people who need me and latch on to people who don't. I dive into every other world except my own just because I want something more glamorous than my real life. I do destructive shit so a stupid hypocritical fish will like me.

I fall for fish instead of girls.

Fuck.

I have to stop and hold my head for a minute, but then I charge forward into the marina and get my shit together.

"I need a fish," I tell the fisherman. "Please."

The one-eyed fisherman leers at me the best he can. I want to run. "Gave you one yesterday," he says.

"Please. My brother's really sick. I can pay. Whatever you need." I take a handful of bills out of my pocket. They're all balled together so I don't have to think about how much it is and how little we will have left. "Please." *Begging you makes me want to kill myself.*

"Still working off a loss today. Come back tomorrow."

I scream. I want to hit him but I know what he'll do to me, and fuck it, I don't care. *"This is a little fucking kid! Give me a fucking fish!"*

The fisherman stares at me, then chuckles a little and turns back to the water.

I want to throw myself into the water, get all caught in his net, do whatever the fuck it takes to make him listen. Make him reel me in and I will scream at him the whole time. I'll grab the fishboy and hold a knife to his throat and tell them what I'll do to their toy if they don't give me a fucking fish.

Fuck.

Fuck me.

I start back to the house. A piece of seaweed flies out of the water and hits me in the cheek. He's not supposed to be here. His dock is ages away.

"Go away," I say. "Not now." I wipe off the salty, slimy trail under my eye.

"Look at me," Teeth says.

I turn around, only because his voice sounds so funny.

He's just about as close to the shore as he can get, his tail fully visible, curled next to him on the sand like a cat's. He holds out a big, plump fish, its neck neatly slit.

He's shaking. His eyes are streaked red. I wasn't even sure that he could cry. He looks like he can't catch his breath.

"I'll get you more if you need," he says. "Take it. Hurry, please. Take it and go. I'll get you another one tomorrow. Is that enough?"

I don't know, but I say "Yes," and I come to him and hold his head between my hands for just a second, because he's still going, "Go. Please go. I need to . . . you have to go," and he's not taking his eyes off that fish.

That night, the screams. God, the screams. Like they're pulling out pieces of him.

Somehow, that one additional fish is enough to tide Dylan over.

fifteen

DYLAN KEEPS HOLDING ON, AND TEETH KEEPS DELIVERING, AND by the next week the fish market is stocked again. This fishboy, I swear.

Everything is all right. My parents are still tentative with Dyl, but they stop watching me like I'm going to jump off the cliffs at any minute. Dylan crashes around in the house again. I feel like I can start going out again.

But things are weird with Diana now, since the fish famine. We don't even talk much anymore. I think that other half of the fish is lying between us. The elephant in the room.

Sometimes we just sit in the library and read together.

It's Tuesday afternoon and I'm bored even with all the books. This hasn't ever happened before. I want to be outside.

Diana turns the pages at three times the rate I do, and lets me sit in the armchair by the window. It faces the water but not the dock. No Teeth from here today.

"The fishermen are hurting him," I tell Diana. "Worse than they used to."

"Interesting."

I want to tell her that she looks like him, but I don't know how to without it sounding like an insult. Who wants to be compared to a fish? I mean, besides Teeth.

As soon as I feel like I've stayed here long enough, I'll head to the dock.

But first I need a break.

"Going to the bathroom," I tell her.

Diana nods and doesn't look up. "Be quiet, remember. Use the one close to my room. My mother has the other one tied up."

I walk down the hallway, the carpet heavy and plush beneath my feet. I've never felt more out of place in my life. I guess this is how Teeth feels.

I can hear Ms. Delaney's cries get louder and louder as I head down the hall. Every Tuesday. Why is she crying? Teeth and Diana both make her sound kind of heartless. She threw her son in the ocean. I'm beginning to hate humans.

There are two doors across the hall from Diana's room. I know one is the bathroom.

Clearly, this was the wrong one.

I'm in a room twice the size of Diana's with bright blue walls and a pale yellow ceiling, a red comforter crumpled over an unmade bed shaped like a race car. The fan is running on the ceiling, like whoever left this room is about to come right back. All the lights are on, even the tiny one on the nightstand painted with stars and moons and the words GOOD NIGHT.

The carpet is even thicker here, where it hasn't been stepped on and worn down. The world's smallest wheelchair is folded up by the foot of the bed, and there's a little bloodred chair in front of the bookshelf.

The whole time it was right here.

The bookshelf. I go to it and there, right on the top shelf, are Mrs. Delaney's diaries. But I don't look. I don't need them anymore.

Instead, I reach for the copy of *Runaway Bunny*. The spine is crumpled like an old piece of paper. Diana's looked barely read.

I open the inside cover, hoping, hoping, and there it is. Blocky left-handed blue crayon letters spell out DANIEL.

Or I could have just looked up, because on the wall, there's a framed embroidery, the same kind my mom made for me when I was born. It has a little train stitched across the bottom and the words DANIEL PETER DELANEY, TUESDAY, JANUARY 2ND underneath.

Oh my God.

"What are you doing in here?"

Oh, fuck. But I turn around, and it's just Diana. Thank God.

Except she doesn't look ready to laugh this off. "What are you doing?" she says again.

"I came in here by accident—"

"Yeah, bullshit you did. Get out."

I take a step back. I don't want to go. "I'm sorry—"

"No. Get out. *Get out of my house.*"

I can't shake the feeling that there's nothing left for me in this house, anyway.

And like she's reading my mind, Diana says as I'm going, in a voice as small as Teeth's when he's sad, "I thought you were here for me."

I'm still panting when I flop down on the dock. Fishboy comes right out from under it, grinning. "Hey!"

"Hey."

"Let's go swimming. I found this cave. *Brand-new.*"

"I'm sure it's been here for a while. Dude, I am in so much shit with your sister."

"New for me, which means new. Come on. Let's go swimming!"

I laugh. I kind of want to, but I'm already freezing just in my jacket. I think being with Teeth keeps me warmer than I logically should be—half-magic, after all—but I don't know if even that's enough to take the bite out of today.

"This cave better be really good. Very, very good."

"It's awesome. It's little, though. And dark."

"It is a cave." And it's already dark out here. I should be getting home. But I don't want to, at all. I need to unwind after all the drama with Diana, and I kind of can't think of anywhere I'd rather be than here.

"Come oooon," he says.

"Do you know how cold it is?"

"Obviously. I'm in the water, aren't I? I'm always cold." He flops on his back and paddles around with his tail.

"Don't give me that shit. Your scales keep you warm."

"Maybe I only told you that so you wouldn't worry about me, did you think of that?"

I laugh. "That would be a new one."

"Come on, Rudy. I won't let you get cold."

I don't know why I listen to him. I thought I'd decided that that was a bad idea. But I'm smiling even while I'm gasping as I lower myself into the water. He's giggling at me, so I smack the top of his head once I'm in.

"You're all shaky!" he says.

"Yeah, it's called shivering."

"I do that sometimes after the fishermen get me. Come on. It's not far."

He swims with me instead of in front of me. He comes up for breath whenever I do, which I think at first is a weird way to be nice, until I notice the deep bruising between two of his ribs. It's the darkest mark I've seen on him.

When we come up again, I pause him with my hand on his arm. "You okay?"

He's panting hard. "What's up with your teeth?" He moves his hand toward my mouth and I stop him.

"They're chattering, and they'll bite you," I say.

"I'll bite *you*."

"You okay?"

"We're really close to the cave, Rudy."

I feel like I'm about to freeze to death in the water, so I nod. "Okay, come on."

He brings me to one of the cliffs and hauls himself out of the water and through a hole. The opening is small. He grabs me by the arm and pulls me up. The ceiling is tall enough for us to sit, but we can't stand up, which I guess is only a problem for me. The floor is the closest thing to real dirt I've felt since we moved here.

"This isn't much, gotta tell you," I say.

"No, no, wait. It gets better." He gets down on his hands and starts to crab walk, dragging his tail behind him.

"You're going to scrape yourself up," I tell him.

"My tail's tough."

Okay. I crawl beside him. He moves more quickly than I expect.

"See?" I tell him. "You'd do fine on land."

"Yeah, just chop my tail off."

"That's kind of an idea, you know?"

"I wouldn't be a fish without my tail, Rudy."

The farther we go into the cave, the heavier and colder the air becomes. I don't think I've ever been this cold, and it's a little scary. I feel like I'm going to need to stop and give up, but that won't help, and the only way to get warm is to swim back to the land, and I don't know how the hell I could do that right now. Too cold. Just too cold.

The cold is aching down to my bones, and I can't hear anything but my teeth chattering.

Fishboy says, "You're moving all over the place."

"I'm shivering."

"Don't be scared."

"I'm not . . ."

"Look. Look up."

I wrap my arms around myself, but it's not helping. I'm just pushing my icy clothes into my skin.

"Look up," Teeth says again. Gently.

I tilt my head up. When did the ceiling get so high?

It's like we've entered some kind of natural ballroom. The ceiling, thirty feet above my head, is dripping with stalactites and bare in places, and moonlight shines down and lights up this shallow pool in the middle of the room. Fishboy crawls his way over to the water and splashes in. "Isn't this place cool? See, you can be on the land and I'll be here, and we're like practically right next to each other. See, I can totally reach you." He touches my hand.

For the first time ever, his hand feels warm. He straightens up in the water. "Damn, Rudy. You're cold."

I try to nod but I can't.

Holy fucking shit, I'm frozen solid.

No, I'm not. I'm breathing. Really slowly, but I'm breathing.

And then his voice changes, and he goes, "Oh, Rudy. You're so cold. Are you okay?"

"I don't know."

"Ummm. Ummmm." He's looking around, his eyes darting from one blank wall to another. "Ummm, okay. Don't worry, Rudy. Don't worry don't worry I'm going to make you okay!"

I close my eyes. My backbone hurts. I'm driving it into the floor with my shivers but I don't even feel cold anymore. I don't feel anything.

"Rudy, *I'll be right back*!" And then he's doing his stupid crawl out of the cavern and right back the way we came.

There isn't even the seed of doubt in my brain. I know he's coming. I keep my eyes closed, and I can see him here already, with blankets or warm clothes or a fucking fire or something, I don't know. Anything that will help. I know he can fix this. I know. I don't know how I know.

Maybe I should have stayed in the mansion.

I know he'll come back, but I'm worried it won't be in time.

No. He'll save me. It's his turn. He would never ever miss his turn. I'm smiling just thinking about it. I'm smiling . . .

I hear the slippery sounds of him sliding back in, and he slurs something, but I can't understand what he's saying. Is that me? Am I dying?

No, it's him. His mouth is full. I watch him come toward me, something glistening in his mouth. Then he spits an Enki onto the ground next to me. "Presents!" He smiles at me and touches my cheek. "Still with me?"

"Uh-huh."

He doesn't even pause before he slits the Enki's throat with his teeth. No tears, no deliberation. He opens up its stomach and takes out a hunk of meat. He moves my jaw up and down to help me chew.

And it's like he's feeding me marshmallows right out of a campfire. I want to close my eyes and fall asleep. I want to be small enough to swim in my mouth, to fill my whole body with this feeling.

He feeds me another bite, and the warmth pricks its way

down to the tips of my fingers. I can sit up a little, and I do. "More."

"Right here." He puts another bite in my mouth. More. There's a soft layer between my clothes and my skin. I'm a blanket right out of the dryer.

"Better?" he says.

"Mmmhmm." I'm praying that he won't stop, and he doesn't. He keeps his eyes locked on the fish while he picks it clean of meat, searching each crevice and around each tiny bone. I can taste the slime on his fingers when he brings them to my lips. It's not as gross as I would have expected—musky, salty, and alive.

By the time he's halfway through, I'm practically okay, but I keep letting him feed me the whole thing. I don't even grab for the meat myself once I can. I let him do it. I want to see if he'll stop. Or break.

He's smiling at me the whole time, bigger and bigger the better I get.

"All done," he says, once the fish is cleaned out. And that's the first moment that he lets go and looks a little sad. And I feel it, warm and heavy, in my stomach.

I grab his wrist and say, "You're incredible," because there's nothing else to say.

Then we're in the pool of water, except really he's in the pool and I'm in the air, because he doesn't want me to get cold. He has me on his shoulders, and he swears it isn't hurting him, swears, and he spins me around and I hold my arms out like I'm flying.

We swim all the way back to the shore like this.

And I spin all the way home.

Mom is staring at me like she doesn't know who I am, but all I'm doing is running around with Dylan on my back. "We're playing airplane," I tell her. I don't know why she looks so surprised. It's not as if I never play with Dylan.

"Must be that new girlfriend," Dad mumbles to her.

I don't know why they think I've changed. It's Dylan. The difference is Dylan, playing back.

I haven't changed. Why would I have changed?

I balance Dylan on my hip while I help Dad with dinner. I realize I'm whistling.

sixteen

THE NEXT DAY ALL THE MAGIC IS GONE, BECAUSE I GO OUT TO
the dock in the morning and Teeth is catching minnows
and mumbling to himself. He's shivering almost as badly
as I was yesterday. I don't know if he's sick or just really
freaked out. He has two black eyes and blood under his
nose. "They broke it?" I ask. "C'mere, let me see."

He doesn't look at me. His eyes keep darting around the
water. "My teeth are doing like yours." They're bending,
they're hitting against each other so hard.

"Yeah. Have you caught anything?"

"Want a catfish . . . They're eating my fish. I saw one of
them eating my fish."

"The catfish are?"

He sneezes so hard it almost knocks him over. "I need to fix my fish. Killed a fish. Need to grow a new fish have a fish can't have babies."

"It's okay."

"Hurt Rudy . . ."

"Whoa." I put my hand on his shoulder. "You didn't hurt me."

"Hurt the fish . . ." He goes back to scanning the water. I touch his forehead, but his skin is just as cold as ever. I don't know what to do. I settle with grabbing the back of his neck and just holding it, the way you'd hold a kitten. He doesn't protest, but he doesn't seem to care much, either. Still, this contact is making me feel better somehow.

A few tunas slide right through his hands, like he can't figure out how to grab them quickly enough. I try to help, and after I practice for a while, I finally grab one, but he doesn't want it. "I want to catch it myself," he whines.

"You're such a kid sometimes, y'know?"

"I'm a fish." He rubs his eyes. "Rudy. Rudy."

"Uh-huh?"

He looks at me and sighs. "I'm really tired."

"Yeah. Let's take a nap."

He used to sleep, he told me a while ago, in a very small cave pretty close to the marina, but the fishermen found him there last week and now he's skittish about going back there. He's okay with letting himself be caught, *sometimes*, for some reason I will probably never understand. But he's clearly really violated that they found his home. I saw it once after a swimming lesson. He had a little piece of net he stole that he used for a pillow and a moldy doll that he found at the bottom of the ocean. I don't know where he's been sleeping since they found him, or where his doll is now.

He wants to go to the sandbar so he can have a bit of him underwater, but I convince him I don't want to freeze again, and that the dock is better because no one can see him. I pull him up there, and he bitches the whole time, but as soon as we're settled he falls asleep with his head on my knee.

He looks so different out of the water. So much smaller, and his scales look dry enough to fall off.

In his sleep he whimpers, and his webbed grip tightens on the calf of my jeans. "Rudy," he whispers, and my throat clenches. In a way it hasn't since Dylan was sick.

"It's okay," I whisper. *I'm right here.*

His hand around my shin is scaring the shit out of me. I can barely move. I don't want to move, and that's so fucking terrifying.

I don't know what I'm going to do. But now I'm shaking too. Fucking fucking Fishboy, what am I going to do?

✦ ✦ ✦

Dad's making cookies downstairs, gingerbread. The burned-sugar smell is mixing with the salty air on its way up the stairs, and my mouth is watering up here in my room. It takes me back to my grandmother's house, when she used to make caramel on the stove and spike it with sea salt.

It's been a streak of warm days, and my window's open. I know it isn't night yet, but I don't hear Teeth screaming, and I let this convince me that everything is okay. Maybe he's still asleep under the dock where I left him.

I wonder if he liked gingerbread when he was a kid.

A breeze rolls into my room. It smells just like the water. I feel calmer than I have in a long time.

seventeen

IT'S TUESDAY AGAIN, AND EVEN THOUGH OUR MEETINGS AREN'T regular like they used to be, it still feels strange not to go up to Diana's in the evening. And I regret it more than I would have thought. I know it's only been a week, but I already feel like I'm forgetting what she looks like or the way her mouth tastes. I miss kissing, but I don't think I miss kissing her.

Maybe that should worry me.

It doesn't. I don't know. Maybe I have too much else to be worried about.

Like the fact that I don't see him on my way to the marketplace, but I hear him now that I'm on my way back. He's moaning my name in between the thrashes of the waves. "Rudy. You motherfucker. Stop waaaaalking. Ruuuuuudy."

"Just a sec." I run the rest of the way home to drop off the groceries. I have a feeling he doesn't want to see my bags full of fish. I can hear him the entire way back to my house, and again the second I step back outside.

"Christ." I get up on the dock. "Where are you?"

"Below you."

I lean over and see the tips of his webbed fingers. I grab his hand and pull him until he floats into the open water. His black eyes have blossomed all the way down his face, and big patches of his scales are missing. I've never seen his tail as mangled as this.

"Shit," I mumble. They found him last night. I thought I hid him well before I left, in that nook by the marketplace. God fucking damn it. He already looked sick last night. He didn't need this now.

He covers his face with his hands and starts moaning, "Rudy," again.

"I know." I want to ask if he's okay, but he's so clearly not okay—the scrapes, the bruises, the tearing at his tail—that I can't ask this the way I mean to without seeming incredibly dense. I know he's not physically okay, but I need to know where my fishboy's brain is right now. I want to know, every time I see him, if they've finally pushed him beyond repair.

How much of this he can actually take before his human brain explodes with human pain.

"Let's go swimming," I say, because I don't know what else to say.

"I'm tired, Rudy."

"I know."

"I'm hungry," he says. Really quietly.

"Have you been floating there all day?"

He nods.

I take a deep breath. "Then get off your ass and catch a fish. You can't just lie around waiting for me all day. Christ, boy. I caught that one catfish and that was just luck."

"You can't even catch a fish with one of those big sticks."

"Fishing poles?"

"Yeah."

"I might have, if you hadn't sliced my line."

He grins, but getting bitched at seems to have given him some energy. He tilts himself up and starts watching the water.

"What did they do to your tail?" I try to ask like I don't really care about the answer, because nothing makes Teeth uncomfortable like feelings that aren't his own. I guess that explains a lot of things I don't say.

"They got bored of my mouth, I guess."

I whisper, "Christ." I don't want to think about it.

He shrugs. "It's what makes me more interesting than a human. You have to use your imagination. Or I don't even exist. I'm a ghooooost." He looks up at me and sticks his tongue out, then dives into the water. He's not as fast as he normally is. He comes up with a foot-long fish in his mouth, grinning at me.

I don't smile. "Why do you do this?"

"What, this?" He slits the catfish's throat. "Kills them faster. It's actually nice of me." He looks at the catfish. "You should be thanking me right now, fishy. Thank your fish king."

"It's dead, babe."

"You know what it is? It's mushy." He holds up some of the meat, making a face. "Look at this. It's mushy. Probably has bugs or something. Taste it. Do you think it has bugs?"

I smack his hand away. "Why do you let them catch you?"

He drops the catfish on the dock and shoves meat into his mouth with both hands.

God. God. I look up at the sky, really just so I don't have to look at him.

He says, "Can't we talk about something else?" And I hear that his throat hurts and he's tired and he wants me here so he doesn't have to think about the other shit. But I can't keep doing this. He was . . . God, he was supposed to be *my* escape. And now he's turning out to be just as much of a nightmare as my fucking family and this fucking island, because I can't fix this. I can't save him.

And even if I could, how many times am I going to have to save this boy who doesn't want to be saved before I finally get it through my fucking head that I can't actually change anything?

God, I'm just the world's shittiest friend.

"Are you mad at me?" he says.

"I don't know."

This clearly wasn't the answer he was expecting, and his face gets dark and his mouth gets small.

"Are you just fucking with me, or what?" I say.

"I'm not fucking . . ."

"Do you even care what happens to you? Do you have to be so goddamn reckless?"

"They're the ones who hurt me!"

"I just don't understand why you don't fight them off. Or swim faster. Or . . . bite harder. Something. I just don't fucking believe that this is something inevitable. Can you honestly tell me that you're fighting as hard as you can?"

He doesn't say anything.

Which is not what I wanted to happen.

Even though I knew it was what was going to happen.

"God*damn* it, Teeth! You know that some people have actual problems, right?"

"*Hey!* Getting whatever—"

"Raped. The word is raped, you stupid fucking fishboy."

That's out of my mouth before I can even think about it.

And I don't care how horrible it is, because what the hell, he can get away and he doesn't.

And some people have actual problems.

He splashes halfheartedly. "It's a big fucking problem, okay?" His throat bobs while he swallows. "It's a big fucking problem."

"But it *doesn't have to be.*"

"What else am I supposed to do?"

"Anything," I say. "Just get away. Please, Teeth."

"And then what?"

"And then you're free."

He throws the catfish carcass into the sea. "Fuck it, Rudy, I'm not free."

"Yeah, because—"

"Shit, boy. Look at me. Do they have me right now? Are you tying me up and hitting me and . . . whatever? Did you trap me?"

"I . . ." I shake my head.

"And do I look free?"

He looks like a lonely kid in an enormous ocean.

He nods up at the dock. "Will you help me get up there?"

"Up here with me?"

"Yeah."

I raise my eyebrows. "I thought the sun hurts your scales."

"Yeah, well. Maybe I'm getting used to it. The salt's hurting the cuts anyway."

I make sure no one's on the beach before I grab him by his elbows and haul him onto the dock next to me. He isn't great at sitting—he has to keep his hands on the dock to brace himself—but he does okay. I can see the rip in his tail more clearly now. A bloody, glistening hole in the middle of his scales.

"Tomorrow I'll bring peroxide to put on that," I tell him.

Teeth touches his black eye and winces. "Look. If they don't catch me . . . what do I do? I swim around my little corner of the ocean, afraid of them forever, wondering all the time if they're coming up behind me. And I free a few fish, but I never free them all—" He looks at me. "You know I know that, right? That no matter what I do, they're bringing fish into market every week?"

I didn't know he knew that.

"You guys aren't dropping dead," he says. "So clearly they're getting the fish out. And I notice when they're gone. I don't know all of them, but . . . you know? Some of them . . . some of them I notice when they're gone." He swallows. I wonder if he knew the one he fed me.

He says, "And then even if by some miracle I managed to stop them, the bigger fish are gobbling mine up all the time, and they're not going to live forever. They're fish. I don't even . . . I don't think fish live very long."

"Yeah. They're fish."

"So I save a few and, in the grand whatever of things, it doesn't fucking matter. I know that. I'm really, really smart, you know?"

I nod a little.

"You don't believe me."

"I believe you."

"You don't even fucking listen to me anymore," he says.

"What are you talking about?"

"You used to think I was cool, and now I'm just this fucking mess that you have to put perox-whatever on. We were . . . It used to be different."

"But . . ." *I can't save you and you can't fix me and I still want to be here and I am scared out of my fucking mind and why won't you get well?*

He picks at the scales he still has until I stop him. When he speaks, his voice is much louder, but he's still not looking at me. "So what's the fucking point of me if I'm not, like, in this battle with the fishermen all the time? If I stop that, what do I do? Float around until I drown? It's not like I can fucking . . . be something. Or even have a real friend."

I wish he'd slapped me instead. "Yeah."

"See, 'cause in a way . . . they're sort of all I have."

I exhale. "The fishermen." And then his hand is in mine, and I don't even know how it got there.

"They're my reason to be here. They're my battle, you know?" He looks at me with a little smile. "And it's not like they do anything I can't handle. I always win. I'm the hero."

"Yeah."

"Yeah." He takes his hand away and dives back into the water. "Look," he says. "Anyway. Operation Fish Freedom Part whatever. You ready?"

I shake my head. I feel like I'm not getting enough air or something, because it's like my head is fuzzy and I can't focus. I think that conversation took too much of me. And it takes me a minute to process where he is. I think I'm still two minutes behind. Eventually I realize what he just asked and say, "Fuck no."

There's no way I'm helping with this, and really, right now I just want to go home. And there's no fucking way I want him going over to the marina today. If he's going to let the fishermen come get him, fine, but he should at least make them work for it. I'm not going to hand-deliver him. I couldn't live with me.

He says, "Come on, Rudy, please?"

Dylan Dylan Dylan, I will not forget Dylan; no way, we're not doing this again.

But I look at Teeth. He's fragile.

Lately I've been thinking *Daniel Daniel Daniel* all the time.

There's no fucking way I'm going with him, but I can at least be gentle. This isn't the time to tell him he's acting like a murderer. So I give him a smile. "I can't tonight.'"

He frowns. "What are you doing?"

"I just have plans."

"With your brother?" His eyes light up a little. "Oh, is he better? Are you going to play with him? Tell him I say hi. Can you play with him out here so I can see?"

"We're still working on getting him better." I say this with a bit of a bite. I can't help it.

Teeth's voice is small. "I'll give you fish after I free them. I promise. Don't get mad."

"That doesn't save everyone else."

"But I can't get fish for all of them. That's . . . that's too many."

How many is too many? I shake my head. "I'm not mad. I just can't tonight. I have plans already. Sorry."

And then he starts screaming. Holy shit. He screams like the sound is coming through the top of his head. No human could ever make that noise.

Then he's gnashing his teeth down so hard that the tips bend. "What? What are you doing? Are you going there?" He waves his hand to the Delaneys' mansion.

"Daniel—"

Oh.

Shit.

I don't know how it happens. I really don't.

He's staring at me, frozen exactly where he was before I spoke, his hand still weakly pointed toward his old home.

And he opens his mouth, and I'm ready for anger and spit and fire, but instead it's just the smallest voice in the world. "What did you call me?"

"I'm sorry. I didn't . . . I'm sorry. Really, I didn't mean to do that."

"Did *she* tell you that?"

"Who?"

"You know who! That girl!"

"No, not really, I—"

"Not really?" He screams again. I just know someone's going to come running out here. Someone has to come. This is not the wind. This is not a ghost. This is the realest thing I've ever seen.

He points his hand at me, his fingers stretched and slimy. "You can't call me that! I didn't tell you you could!"

"I know. I'm sorry."

"You can't hurt me with that!"

"I didn't say it to—"

"I don't even care if she told you." He shakes his head hard. "I don't care what she told you. You know why? You want to know why I don't care?"

I can't take this. I feel meaner every time he speaks.

He says, "Because I don't care what you do. I don't care

what you do at all, Rudy! Go hang out with humans. I don't care. I can do all of this on my own."

"No, you can't. Please don't go to the marina. Don't free the fish. Not tonight. Come on. You're tired. You're probably sick. Stay here and rest. Eat another catfish."

It's like he didn't even hear me. "I don't care if you hang out with humans. I hate humans. Go make out with my sister. Whatever. I bet her lips are, like, warm and stuff."

I exhale. "She has nothing to do with this."

"Bullshit!" He splashes hard with his tail. "You think I don't see you going up to the house instead of coming down here to be with me?"

"I can't be with you all the time!"

He glares at me. His eyes are as shiny as the surface of the water.

I say, "I don't go over there that often. But she doesn't leave the house, you know? She gets lonely."

"I get lonely! *I get lonely, you asshole!* I hate humans!"

"What do you expect me to do? Fuck! You can't just stand there—"

"*Stand* here?" His mouth hangs open. "Did you just say *stand* here?"

"—and fucking scream at me because you finally figured out you're not my whole world."

"Fuck your world! Fuck you and your human names your mom gives you and your brains and your lungs and your everything, because I don't need any of it! This isn't your world anymore! Take a look at where you are, asshole." He splashes me with a webbed hand full of water. It's so cold it burns. I scoot back.

"You can't handle being fucking splashed!" He says, "You can't even handle being here if I don't keep you safe."

"Yeah, let's not talk about who's saving who."

"This is *my* world!"

Except it isn't his world. It's the fish's world. And he's not a human, but he's not a fish, either. And it's all crushing him and I don't know what to do because I guess I'm not even a real friend or something.

And he goes, "I don't even know your world," and fuck, he better not cry.

Because I don't know what to do. I invited him to live in my house, for fuck's sake. That was the furthest I could go. How much of me does he seriously think is available right now?

I have other shit.

I close my eyes and breathe as deeply as I can. "Teeth . . ."

What does he want me to do, grow a tail and swim with him forever? Forget about my family?

I won't let myself picture it. I won't think about it. I won't imagine how nice the water must feel in the summer.

Because it's impossible. So there's no point in thinking about it. There's no point in looking at him and wondering . . . because it just doesn't make sense.

And thinking this truth hurts, because pretending I didn't know it was so easy.

"I am so pathetic," I whisper.

He mumbles, "I'm a fish."

I guess he doesn't know what pathetic means.

I need to get out of here. My lungs feel like they're pushing through my rib cage, and where he splashed me is still stinging. And I don't even know if we're arguing anymore, but we're staring at each other like there's so much more we need to say, but he doesn't know the words and I am not going to be the one to say it.

Because I have enough shit going on right now, and he was supposed to be the easy part.

And I might throw up.

I need to get out of here, but I can't leave him like this. So I say, "Don't you fucking dare go down to the marina on your own, okay? I mean it."

And then he just snaps. "You don't tell me what to do! Don't you ever tell me what to do again! I hate humans!" He pushes off the dock and swims away.

I don't stop him.

I shouldn't give a shit that he's going. That they're probably going to catch him and beat him hard before they let him go. It shouldn't matter to me. He's just a fish.

I run into my house, ignoring my parents, who for some reason choose tonight to demand to know where I've been and why I'm all wet, and I run up to my room and I scream. And I'm ripping pictures off the walls—not even the pictures of him, because those are all hidden away—the ones of my family, my parents and my fucking fucking fucking brother, and I'm breaking my lamp because I threw it and I'm screaming.

And over the ocean, which started screaming and thrashing when I did, which knows exactly how fucked up this is, which is trying to swallow the fishboy before someone else swallows him, no one can even hear me, and no one even has any idea.

But I can hear him.

The ocean might be louder tonight than I've ever heard, roaring and growling, but I sleep right through it. I only wake up for the train whistle scream, the shriek of sharp teeth gnashed together, the hoarse warble from deep in his throat. The word please.

Magic word.

The silence.

It's just the wind. It was just the wind, and it's dying down now.

It's nothing. It's just this ghost of this boy who used to be.

I skip breakfast to go out early with peroxide, because I don't have anything else to bring for a peace offering. And

I can't just walk around feeling like this, like I've swallowed a bucketful of sand. If that means I need to grovel, then fine, I'll fucking grovel.

Because there's always someone who's more powerful, and ever since Teeth fed me that fish, it's become really clear which one of us will sacrifice more than the other.

They better not have hurt him too badly.

"Teeth?" I get up on the dock and wait for him to come out.

He doesn't.

eighteen

IT GETS COLD ENOUGH TO MAKE OUR FIRST FIRE. DAD'S WORRIED about the smoke and Dylan's lungs, but he does really well. I think he's happy I've been at home more. He glues himself to my lap and talks my ear off about the starfish he found on the shore this morning while he was out in the sand with Mom.

I know that even if Teeth were out in the water, he would have hidden from Dylan and Mom, so the fact that Dyl doesn't mention him shouldn't bother me. I shouldn't even think about it. I shouldn't even notice, really.

Dylan falls asleep, eventually, with his head against my shoulder. Dad goes into the kitchen to do dishes, and I can tell by the way Mom's eyes track him that she wants to follow. She has this crazy look on her face like Dad is really attractive all of a sudden. Maybe it's that everything has been so calm, all day—all week, even—and she can finally think about sex. It should gross me out, but I just think it's kind of funny. My parents' sex life is so incredibly far from having anything to do with me.

She looks at me and nods at Dylan, her eyebrows up. I mouth, "We're fine." She kisses the top of my head on her way to the kitchen. I hope she at least waits until she's out of earshot before she pounces on him.

The ocean hits the rocks like a bomb, but Dylan doesn't wake up.

I'm trying to figure out something else to think about, so my brain will shut up, *TeethTeethTeeth*, so I keep myself focused on Dylan as hard as I can. After a minute of this, I'm totally zoned in, like Dylan is the only thing in my whole life. The weight he's gained makes him soft against my chest. I feel him breathing into my neck. I'm watching this spot on the back of his head where his hair's a little thinner than the rest like it's the prettiest painting in the world.

It's hitting me that I have no idea what the hell I am to this kid.

There are eleven years between us. It's not like we were ever really expected to play together. And I'm only just starting to accept the idea of him as a real person, and not a toddler in a hospital bed with bad lungs and the world's softest cry.

I hold him a little tighter.

But can I be free? Can I get up without waking him up?

I'm tasting the salt and the wind and the great big ocean and no no no, not that kind of free. Home. Think about going home.

No. Dylan. We're thinking about Dylan.

I want Dylan to be more than just how Dylan makes me feel. And I'm starting to get that he is. He's here. He got well.

And now I guess I need to.

I'm still here about an hour later, when he wakes up and complains that I'm all sweaty and so gross and why won't I put him down? And I pick him up and spin him around.

I guess I'll figure it out. It looks like he's going to be around for a long time.

And for a minute I'm warm. And I'm really not thinking about anything but Dylan, because he isn't some abstract concept anymore. He's this smile and these hands on my cheeks. Dylan.

It's a windy night, and the water is loud and vicious and whipping against the dock. My parents fell asleep with Dylan in their bed, all of them curled into a ball.

I yell, *"Fishboy!"*

The ocean responds like a clash of thunder.

Screaming.

It's at a lower pitch than before. Usually, he's a whistle. Tonight he sounds like a boy.

I can't see the marina from here. I should run down. I need to run down. I need a better reason not to run down besides that I'm so fucking scared.

"Teeth!"

Okay, so he isn't the world's best. In fact, he's pretty much a total asshole, and he's the biggest hypocrite in the world, and he thinks fish count as much as humans and whether or not that's true it's not something that can fit into my life right now, and he doesn't even try to accept that, but he's *my* total asshole and I can't just leave him alone. That is not how this is going to work.

He deserves to be free.

I'm crying all of his names.

I can't see the marina, but all I can picture is them ripping at him and crumbling him, and I don't understand how he could let this happen.

Or how I could let this happen. Or why I can't be a good friend to anyone in the whole world.

I don't go to the marina.

nineteen

THE NEXT DAY, TUESDAY, TEETH STILL ISN'T BACK, SO WHEN Mom offers to go to the marketplace with me, I tell her no, I'll go alone, it's no problem.

She looks at me with a silly smile. "Just don't take too long getting home."

"I'm just walking down and then back."

"Huh. I thought you'd want to stop by the house to spend some more time with your girlfriend."

"Oh. Diana."

"But you can't marry her, promise me. We'd have the same name."

Get me out of here.

"Yeah, I, uh, anyway, I think she can spare me for the morning."

Mom smiles and kisses my cheek on my way out. I feel dirty for reasons I don't want to think about.

I run to the marketplace.

So here's what I'm hoping. I want enough fish so that I can get some for Dylan without trouble, but I want there to be a few less than usual, so I'll know that Teeth has been gone all this time because he's freeing more fish. He's getting away. Maybe they catch him, but he has time to get out and breathe, but then he goes back in because he might be an asshole, but fuck, he's brave.

So that's what I want to see. Enough fish, but slightly fewer than usual, and I won't have to worry about anything.

I'm early, and the fishermen aren't here yet. I wave to a few people, then help Sam set up his bottles of milk. He gives me one for free in return.

Fiona is standing by the cliffs, looking into the water. I go over and stand with her, say hi.

She smiles at me. Her lips are dry, and they curl over her gums.

The fishermen hike up the hill, their boots squishing against the skin. They approach their stand and grin at us with gold teeth.

And they unload more fish than I've ever seen. Heaps and heaps of fish.

Fuck.

They have him.

I know I need to buy a few before I go, but I'm not sure I should be going anywhere near the fishermen right now. I might do something horrible if I do. Horrible for my family, at least.

I stay where I am, right next to Fiona. "The ghost isn't with me," I say to her.

She looks at me, her brows furrowed together.

I say, "I'm scared."

"Where is the ghost?"

"Trapped."

She nods. "The ghost is always trapped."

"No, not trapped like this."

She keeps nodding. "The ghost will always be trapped."

"Why?"

"You just said it, didn't you?" She's looking at the water again. "Because you are scared."

No fucking way. Not this time. "Thanks, Fiona." I kiss her cheek and run to the fish stand. I throw my money down before I start wondering if I can kill someone with a paper cut to an artery. Leave them, Rudy. Leave them. I grab two handfuls of fish. One is still flapping weakly.

"Hey!" the one-eyed fisherman says.

"I don't need them wrapped." I swallow the instinct to say thank you. I stuff the naked fish into my bag. I run.

I need to find him. I need to find him. Holy shit, I need to find him before they get back. They must have him tied up. He has to be trapped somehow, or he would get away. I have to believe that he would get away.

One of the fishermen will be back soon; they never both stay at the market together for more than a few minutes. Once they're done unloading, one will return and get back to work.

I'm too scared to call out. Too worried he won't answer.

I scan the area as quickly as I can. The rowboats are both empty, save a pile of nets in one and a few spare fishing rods in the other.

I check underneath the boats. I better not find a body. He was screaming just last night. They couldn't have killed him. No way. No fucking way.

I dig through a pile of nets. Nothing. I run toward the shrimp boat, that unused rickety thing. And there he is. I see the tip of a tail, tattered and bloody, peeking out from the inside of the cabin. If I didn't know better, I'd never know it was anything but a bit of a discarded fish.

I'm inside. "Teeth." It's too dark for me to see anything, but I feel some part of him underneath my hand. It's sticky and cold. Maybe his stomach.

He makes a noise, and I can tell both that he's alive and that he's been gagged.

"Okay. Okay, shh." I try to crawl my hands up him to figure out where his face is, but there are so many ropes and so much blood. Fuck, I wish I could see him. I'm never going to be able to get him out of here in the dark.

I'm going to need to leave him and come back.

I find his face, finally, and tug the gag out of his mouth. He says, "Rudy Rudy Rudy," over and over, his voice scraping all the way up to the roof of his mouth.

"Listen to me," I say.

He's quiet. I hear his chest growling when he breathes.

"Do you remember, in the cave, when you told me you would come back?"

"Uh-huh." I hear his voice right on the edge of tears, and I also hear, behind me, the squishing noise of boots coming down the hill.

So I say, "I'll be back," as fast as I can, and I kiss his forehead before I can think of anything better to do. I'm out of there in a second, covered in his blood, and I grab my bags and scale the cliffs like a fucking master. Then I'm straight down the beach, into the water, washing myself clean. So cold, but the water is gentle, licking at the wounds that aren't mine.

I come out and reclaim my bags. That fish that was wiggling isn't anymore. The smallest one. I take him out and hold him. I stare into his eyes that don't look anything like Teeth's.

"Hey, it's okay," I tell him, even though he doesn't speak English. "It's all good. I'm going to save your brother."

It takes me longer than it should to come up with a plan. I don't know if that's because the situation has warped my thought process, or if I'm just trying to avoid my only real option.

Or maybe it's just because, to be lame and honest, what I really want to do right now is run to my parents and have them fix everything. But they don't know about Fishboy, and I don't think they'd be too pleased about saving the boy responsible for the fish shortage that nearly destroyed us.

There's only one person in the world I can think of who can help me save him.

And the more I think about it, the more I realize there's absolutely no way I can do this without her.

Diana takes a while to answer, so I'm practically throwing myself at the door by the time she gets there. "What do you want?" she says.

"I need help."

"Oh yeah?"

Deep breath. "I need your mom's gun."

She raises her eyebrows, but not like she's surprised, just like she's ready for me to tell her more. Whenever I'm around Diana, I get the sense she's already planned everything out, right down to what I'm going to say at every minute.

But I still feel like my tongue's in my throat whenever I talk to her. Maybe my feelings about her aren't as complicated as I thought. I really am easy.

"I'm not going to kill anyone," I say. "Just wave it around threateningly or whatever."

"And then have a lovely life in prison."

"That . . . won't happen." I've only let myself glance over that thought. It's a rule I made up a minute ago.

"Why not?"

"I don't know."

Fuck. How do people in movies do this? No one in movies ever goes to prison, unless they're a bad guy. This is a rescue mission. So everything has to work out.

I say, "Look, the fishermen have Daniel. We . . ." And then my chest is spasming when I try to talk. It feels awful. "They caught him trying to free the fish, and they've been hurting him really badly lately, and now he's tied up and he's just . . . he's gagged and he's bloody and he can't get away, and they're probably going to kill him if he stays there any longer, and we can't just let him die. Or worse, and we can't just . . ."

Her eyebrows are still up.

"And he's your brother," I say. "You can't let your brother die."

"I've never even met him."

But . . . he's her brother. That means something. It always means something.

"He's my best friend." Even I know now that this feels like the wrong word for what Teeth and I are. But it's the only way I can convince her to come.

"You're just *using* me," she says.

"It's not that." Or maybe it is. "I need you." At least that's true. Right now I need her. That isn't what she wants, but it's all I can say right now besides I need him, and that isn't going to win me any points with her, I don't think.

She says, "This doesn't change the fact that you'll rot in prison. Assault with a deadly weapon. That's a major offense." She nods.

"I'm not going to assault anyone."

"Well. There's only one solution."

And she's going to say that we let the fishermen keep him.

She's going to ask how long fishboys live, anyway, tell me that it isn't forever.

She's going to say that they'll just catch him again tomorrow, and what's the fucking point.

She's going to say that nothing is ever going to change.

"I'll have to come with you," she says, with a heavy sigh.

I look at her.

"I have an overinflated sense of justice. I've read Harry Potter too many times." She shrugs. "And I'm already in prison."

If my friends or my girlfriend back home saw who I've turned into, I don't think they'd recognize me.

And I think that's okay with me.

twenty

THE OCEAN IS QUIETER TONIGHT. THE WAVES RUSHING UP TO the shore sound like whispers. I'm standing on the dry sand, and it's freezing cold and rough on my bare feet. I remember when I was a kid, and I learned that glass was made from sand. I thought that was crazy. Now I feel like there are millions of bits of frozen pieces of glass right underneath me.

I'm looking up at the mansion to see if she'll come. I have a flashlight, and Diana is bringing the gun. Except she's never been out of the house at night before.

Part of me is sure she'll chicken out But this is a kid who grew up on stories of orphans slaying dragons. I don't think anyone in the world is less aware of her limitations than Diana. Maybe going outside isn't something she can't do, it's just something she hasn't done yet. Just like saving a mermaid. This is a big experiment, testing a life she's been considering pursuing since she opened her first book.

And then she steps out the front door and begins her way down the stairs, like she's done this every night for years. Her head is up, the gun dangling from her hand.

She looks down at me and smiles. It's a little shy, a little flirty. A bit of the ocean licks my feet.

She takes a step off the bottom of the stairs and stops. "What?" I say.

"The tide's up."

I want to tell her about sand and glass, but I'm sure she already knows. She knows everything.

She looks at the ocean. Then she squeezes her eyes shut, like she's trying to remember. But she isn't.

I say, "We have to go," as gently as I can. I want to say, "It won't hurt you," but God, I don't know. I've seen the ocean be quite the asshole since I moved, and the fact that I'm not afraid of it anymore doesn't really mean it's safe.

"Right." She smiles and kisses me. "Right, Rudy. Of course." She doesn't touch the water, and she stays on the side of me that's farther from the incoming waves.

We walk to the marina together, and she puts her hand that isn't holding the gun into mine. It doesn't really feel right, but it does feel very good. Her hand is so warm.

I almost laugh, thinking about what my parents think Diana and I do together. The kiss was so chaste. Something's over.

"Remember," she says, "I'm not killing anyone." She made the executive decision that she's going to be the one to wield the gun. I don't know.

"Of course. No killing anyone."

"I'm only threatening."

"Don't shoot any fish, either. Teeth'll freak out, and it's really no good to have him freaking out right now."

"Why would I shoot a fish?" She thinks about this for a minute. "Can I shoot one if it tries to rape me?"

I swallow. "Yeah. Yeah, shoot anything that tries to rape you, definitely."

"But not the fishermen."

"I mean, if they try to . . ." I shake my head. "Don't shoot the fishermen. We need the fish."

"I know, Rudy."

But her answer doesn't stop the soreness in my stomach. Lightning strikes way off in the distance, over the sea. It's so far away that we don't hear the thunder, but I can taste the electricity, or I feel like I can. It tastes like the sour candy Mom used to hand out on Halloween. It tastes like cigarettes.

Diana says, "Are we going?" and points the way with her gun.

I hadn't realized I'd stopped. "Right." We walk, together, the rest of the way to the marina.

We crouch behind the rocks and peer around the corner.

No sign of the fishermen. Now I remember that I have no idea where they sleep. Fuck. I should have looked for pillows and blankets or hammocks or something last time I was here. And it's too dark now to see much of anything, and it's not like I'm about to go waving my flashlight around. I'm not turning it on until I'm in the cabin.

"I don't know where the fishermen are," I say.

Diana whispers, "Maybe they have houses."

I shake my head. "We're the only house this far over." And I think I know who lives in every other house on the island. I wish Teeth were with us. He knows for sure where everyone lives.

"Where is he?" she asks.

I point toward the boat.

"Well," she says. "Come on then."

I feel like this is too easy. I guess the hard part will be keeping him safe after we get him free. No, I can't think that far ahead right now. I need to focus. And then I'll hide him under my bed or something, I don't fucking care. I'll worry about that later.

I lead the way while she walks behind me, turning in half circles with the gun outstretched. She must have read a heist book, because she's really good at this. I bet she could shoot to kill.

I climb into the boat and into the cabin. "Hey, champ,

I'm back." I switch on the flashlight and blink a few times, and then everything comes into focus.

His arms are tied up and behind his head, and a long spike holds the base of his tail to the floor. Most of the scales on the front of his tail are missing. There are just a few left, clinging to the bloody ulcers right above the tip of his tail. The hole at the top, the one that used to be so small that you could almost believe it was innocent, now goes almost all the way through him, and it's weeping a million different shades of fluid. His whole body is bloated from swelling.

And I think, *I'm too late.*

I left him for too long.

His face is mostly bruises. I take out the gag.

I whisper, "Teeth?"

And he opens his eyes, squinting in the light, and gives me the world's faintest smile. "Not anymore," he says, with a small laugh. He opens his mouth wide.

All his teeth are filed down to almost nothing.

I start with the spike on his tail.

Diana is standing guard at the door, but I still get freaked out every time Teeth moans. "You've got to be quiet, kiddo," I say. "You've got to be quiet. Do you know where they sleep?"

"No." He breathes hard, the remains of his teeth mashing together. I hear the dangling flakes that cling to the stubs, thin like shale, clicking and breaking off, and it makes me feel sick.

He cries out as I edge the spike farther out. I consider putting the gag back in his mouth, but, just, no, so instead I keep one gentle hand on him while the other is pulling out the spike and pray it's enough to keep him calm. He whimpers.

"Shhhh. I know."

"It's not fair, you know?"

"I know."

"You've saved me way more times than I've saved you."

Oh. "You tend to get yourself in more shit than I do."

"Not a good friendship."

"Well. We're not exactly friends." I give him a smile so he'll know I'm kidding. This smile feels like the worst thing I've ever done.

But he grins. "Look at that big smile. Knew you were an asshole."

I twist the spike out a little farther, and he groans. "I know," I say.

He's not grinning anymore. Every time I move the spike, he sobs again. He looks so dried up, but a few tears find their way out.

"They changed the game," he says.

"I know. But we're changing it too."

"Can't do this again, Rudy."

"I promise." But I have to stop there because my heart is

beating so hard it's shaking my whole chest, and it's hard to talk, especially when I don't know how to finish my sentences.

A few seconds later the spike is out. The wound doesn't look as bad as the one farther up on his tail. Probably because this one hasn't been agitated as much. I have to keep swallowing so I don't throw up, or say something I shouldn't, but the words "I'm really sorry" come out before I can stop myself.

I can tell he wishes I had. "Man, shut up and fucking untie me." He sounds so different without the teeth.

I dig through the fishermen's stuff until I find a knife, and I start working on his wrists. "Diana, anything?"

"No," she whispers.

"Who's Diana?" Teeth mumbles. He sounds like he's falling asleep.

"Your sister." I smack his cheek. "Stay with me now. We'll sleep later. I'll bring you home and you can sleep on my couch."

He snickers for a minute, then stops and creaks open one eye. "My sister?"

"Yeah. Don't get excited. I mean your human sister."

"I know . . ." But he must not be processing it, because he still looks like he gives a shit.

"She's our girl with a gun tonight," I say, and he seems to wake up even more.

"Diana sounds like Daniel," he says, and then he shakes his head a little and goes, "Gun?"

Diana says, "Rudy, I heard something."

Fuck. "We're almost done."

I finish slicing through the ropes around Teeth's wrists, and before I can even announce to him that he's free, he crashes into me, his head against my chest, his arms curled up around himself and pressing into me. I can feel his heart beating, so much lighter than mine, so fast that it reminds me of a hummingbird from back home. He shoves his face into my chest, which must hurt his bruises, but he keeps pushing all of himself harder and harder against me, like every time he comes a little closer, he thinks it will be close enough, but it isn't.

Shit.

I don't know what to do besides whisper, "It's okay," because the fishermen are coming and it's the middle of the night and he's bleeding all over me and he's a fish and I'm a boy and Diana and . . . shit.

"Rudy!" Diana hisses.

I put Teeth on the floor. "Stay here."

"No no fuck no you can't leave me here."

"And you can't swim on your own, so you have to wait for us. It's going to be fine. I'm gonna be right back." There isn't any other choice.

I scramble out the door. "We have to carry him out of here."

"I want to see him. . . ."

"Yeah, come on."

Above us there's a heavy clomp of two pairs of boots, and the fishermen come down the stairs to the boat's main deck.

They were asleep right above us, and we didn't even notice.

Shit.

"Well." The one-eyed one sneers at us. "What do we have here?"

Diana raises the gun and holds it out with both hands. "We have this."

For a second I'm afraid they're not going to care. That they're going to laugh and bend up the barrel of our gun, twist it into a knot, tell us that we are children and fish and they are humans and this is a world so much bigger than we will ever understand. They will pull the earth out from under us and show us exactly, stroke for stroke, what they did to the fishboy, and we will not be able to breathe.

Instead they freeze, their eyes huge. The fat one eventually croaks, "Look, lady. We don't want any trouble."

"No, *you* look," she says. "We're taking the fishboy. And you're going to stand here and let me do it. Or you're both going to taste your own brains." She aims at the one-eyed one's mouth.

I guess that's from a book.

The fishermen grunt stuff about how that's fine, they don't care, there's no need for any of this, they found him in the water a few days ago and they were just trying to keep him from stealing their fish, they don't need him, they don't want him. They don't need him.

Diana doesn't take her eyes off the fishermen when she says, "Can you get him on your own?" It takes me a minute to realize she's talking to me.

"I think so." I crawl back into the cabin. "Hey, you."

"Hey." He's shaking. I should have stayed in here with him and let Diana handle them. She's on top of this.

"Ready to go?" I say.

"They don't *need* me?"

"Don't worry about that. Come on. We're going."

"Never coming back." He raises his arms and helps me pick him up. When I get him outside, the fishermen leer and the fat one smacks his lips, but they don't make any moves toward him. Teeth shivers nonetheless and puts his face into my shoulder.

"Let's get out of here," I say. I touch Diana's arm. Teeth looks up to watch my hands. I don't know what he's thinking, but his grip on me suddenly tightens, and he's tugging that arm back over to wrap around himself.

Oh.

He brings his eyes up for just a second to look at Diana. He yanks my sleeve. "I want her to look at me."

"Later, okay?"

"Now."

I guess this isn't the time to argue with him. Diana hands

me the gun. I'm a lot more awkward with it than she was, but I keep it stretched out in front of me and I keep my face fierce. I'll let them have their moment.

"Hey," I hear Diana say.

And he says, "How's Mom?" They both laugh weakly. I guess that was a joke.

Diana says, "Rudy, let's go. He probably needs medical attention." She's talking like a textbook like she sometimes does. I kind of love that.

I let my hand brush against hers when I give the gun back. Teeth stares. I say, "Yeah, the mermaid hospital. We'll clean him up as best we—"

Then Teeth grabs the gun.

He studies it for a minute, with his finger on the trigger, and mumbles, "Just like in *Bambi*."

He straightens his arm toward the fishermen and methodically shoots each of them in the head.

I hear running footsteps as they hit the ground. I'm confused, and I think one of them has somehow survived and fled, or that Teeth has grown the legs he needs and started to run, thank God, far, far, so far away, but then I realize the fishboy is still in my arms and it's Diana running as hard and as fast as she can toward her house, not looking back, and the blood is pooling at my naked toes.

I guess this was too real for her.

Because God fucking knows it's too real for me.

twenty-one

I MANAGE TO LOWER TEETH TO THE DOCK BEFORE I START throwing up.

"Whoa, what are you doing?" Fishboy leans forward and watches me. "That's so cool. Do it again!"

I do.

"Man, that's awesome. I wish I could do that. Can I do that?"

I grab him by his shoulders. *"You fucking killed them!"*

He's grinning like I just told him I'm buying him ice cream. "They went down so *fast*. They didn't even get to say anything. I wonder what they would have said. Killed by a fish!"

I let go of him. "Christ, Fishboy!"

The smile's gone. He stares at me. He's the world's most battered child. "My name is Teeth."

I think I'm going to puke again, but I don't.

"You're mad at me?" he says.

I back away from the dock and pace on the sand. My chest feels like it's breaking into pieces.

And the fucking ocean, the ocean is so quiet, because I guess the fucking ocean just doesn't know how to act appropriately for anything, goddamn it, the fucking ocean, I am so sick of the fucking ocean and I don't know what to do and I want to dive in and get clean and never have to come back out. I want to stay underwater forever and plug my ears and . . .

And I guess I just wish the storm way out at sea would come closer, just so I would have something to think about besides the two fucking fishermen wrecked into pieces in the marina.

"I can't believe you did that," I say. "That you even could do that."

"They hurt me."

I can't look at him.

"They hurt me!" Fishboy says again, louder, and fine, fine, I look up, and he's raised himself off the dock as much as he can, resting on the bottom of his tail. "Look at me!"

I look.

Christ, half of his scales are gone. I don't know how he's balanced as well as he is when the bottom of his tail is that ripped. I don't know if he's ever going to swim well again. One of his eyes is swollen all the way shut. Half of his hair is matted down with blood. I need to wash him clean.

The fact that my brain is saying, right now, that I need to wash him clean, tells me that those men got exactly what they deserved.

I breathe out.

"I know." I get back on the dock. "I know." I want to touch him, but it's like I can't figure out how. My fingers keep twitching away. I eventually touch the swollen eye, really carefully, and he leans a little in to my hand. And it's okay.

I take a handful of seawater and carefully rinse out the cuts on his face. He winces and looks down. "You got a scrape," he says. "On your knee."

"Yeah? I don't know how." Probably getting down on the ground too quickly when I first saw him. Or crashing onto the dock to let him go.

He leans down and cups his hands for water and rinses my scrape. It hurts more than it helps, but I let him do it anyway. Then I figure I should probably leave his cuts alone until I have something besides saltwater.

"I'm sorry," I whisper.

He says, "You didn't do anything," in this voice that knows that I did. He exhales and looks out to sea for a minute.

"You don't have to talk about it," I say, but really I'm just not sure if I can stand to listen.

"They fucking hurt me this time."

I need to do something. I wonder where I put that peroxide. Fuck. "I know."

He shivers, hard and fast, like a spasm. Then he gags.

I say, "You're going to do that cool thing that I just did, now."

He laughs a little, but he doesn't throw up. He presses his slimy palms into his eyes. "They kept bringing in these loads of fish and dumping them right next to me. I think they caught more fish this week than they usually do in a month, without me free and being a whatever."

"Vigilante." It occurs to me that I could feed him a fish and he might be good as new, but somehow I don't think he'd go for that. He's not an idiot. He knew the fish would fix hypothermia, he knows if they could fix this. There's no way it's worth it to him. He'd kill one to save me, but not to save himself. Just like I'd risk Dylan's life for him but not for me. It makes us a little horrible.

"Fucking assholes," he says. "Going to fish them all away. Then what?" He exhales. "Then what do I do? What am I even supposed to do here, no fishermen and no fish?" He looks at me in a way that might mean something.

But my throat just dropped down to my chest.

Teeth watches me. "What's wrong?"

"Holy shit."

Dylan.

Fishermen.

Dead.

Dead.

"Dylan," I manage to say.

"Your brother?" He lights up, just like every time, then I see him go through exactly the same process I just did, and his eyes go out and his cheeks drop and he bites his lip. "Oh."

"Yeah. Oh."

Holy fucking fucking fucking shit.

What have I done?

I'm staring at Teeth like I don't know who he is.

"There will be more fishermen," he says. "There are always more fishermen."

"In the next week?" No one knows the fucking bait. Fuck. Fuck.

He doesn't say anything.

Fuck. I can't believe what I did. I went in recklessly and didn't even think about how my family would get fish after I threatened the fishermen at gunpoint. And I didn't think, for a second, what we were going to do if things went so incredibly wrong.

I say, "What are we going to do?"

"I don't know."

"What did you *do?*"

"I can try to catch fish for you—"

"You can't swim!"

"I have to swim!" His voice breaks. "I'm a *fish!*"

"What were you thinking? You killed two people!"

"I don't give a shit! Stop yelling at me!" He folds up and puts his head in his lap. "Stop yelling at me!" he says again, breathing so hard. "I hate them and I hate humans and I hate you and I don't fucking care, and if you say one more word about your fucking brother, I'm going to scream so loud that my throat falls out and I'm going to tell everyone I exist and that you killed the fishermen!"

I stare at him. This bruised and bloody fish I don't recognize.

"I don't care," he says. "I don't care about the fishermen and I don't care about my stupid human sister and I don't care about you and I don't care about your brother." He looks at me. "I'm a *fish.* I'm a heartless mean king of the fish and I don't care about you and I don't care about anything! I'm *strong!*" He's shaking like it's the only thing he knows how to do. "I'm so *strong!* Nobody hurts me. Nobody can hurt me. This is my game and I didn't do anything wrong and I'm just trying to help and it's not my fault, I didn't do anything, they hurt me, and *I hate this.*"

And then for a minute, just a minute, my brother fades from me, for one more minute I can't spare, but I can't help it. I know what I need to think about, and I'm not thinking about it. I'm thinking about Teeth. All I see is him.

This bruised, bloody boy I know too well.

And he's staring at me like he knows everything in my entire head.

Maybe he does.

And maybe he has a right to be angry about it. Because he has been raw and I have been guarded, and all this time I thought he was manipulating me. Now look at us.

"I don't feel anything," he insists, his voice so weak.

So I'm crashing into him, and my arms are all the way around him, and he's so small and shivering and I'm holding him as hard as I can, and just when I think he's about to crack and say the three words I don't know how to deal with, he whispers, "I hate humans," and he's crying as hard as I've ever seen.

And I feel everything.

In the morning I wake up not to screams, but to shouting from the marina. But most of the town, I find out, is gathered in the marketplace, swearing and crying and putting up posters calling for a midnight hunt of the sea monster who killed the fishermen.

Fuck.

She told.

twenty-two

MY MOTHER HAS RUSTED COMPLETELY OVER.

Dad is throwing things and screaming about what kind of world do we live in where there are sea monsters; why can't we rely on anything—medicine, reality, morality, my brother—to be real, and what the fuck are we going to do, how the fuck are we going to go on?

Dylan is still totally healthy, hidden in his room, and we're already planning his funeral. I'm sitting at the kitchen table with my eyes closed, thinking about colors of flowers.

And Mom doesn't talk to anyone.

Dad eventually decides that the sea monster story has to be bullshit, that someone else killed them and is using the sea monster as an excuse. All we have is Ms. Delaney's gun, the one she said she threw in the ocean years ago, next to the fishermen on the marina.

All we have is gooey residue on the gun's handle.

I go down to the marketplace to try to barter whatever I can, to get out of the house, but nobody has any fish they'll give me. And after ten minutes around the town square, I'm convinced Dad's the only one who isn't sure the sea monster is a murderer. I buy milk. Most of the shops are closed, and everyone is leaning against the booths and the doors of the nearby houses plotting rigs with the fishing nets and shooting sprees with hunting rifles. One man rests against the door of the rundown firehouse, sharpening a knife twelve inches long.

"You're losing the ghost," Fiona tells me. "Finally."

"The ghost is with me," I tell her, and she shakes her head. "He is," I insist.

"The ghost is finished," she says. And I get so freaked out by that that I run to the dock. But he isn't dead. I see him floating on his back asleep under the dock, and I hang my head over the edge and watch his chest rising and falling. He isn't gone, not even a little. I don't wake him up, because I know he'll want me to hang around, and I can't stand to tell him right now that the whole island's against him. I don't know what I'm going to tell him.

And I need to be getting home.

We have three days of fish stored up, and then God knows what we're going to do. Recovering Teeth to the point that he can catch fish isn't even a semivalid choice anymore, since I honestly can't picture him surviving much longer with everyone looking for him. Shit, I can't think about this.

The truth is that we're fucked. I drank all the milk on the way home, but no one even notices.

"What's wrong with Mom?" Dylan asks me.

"She's just sad."

"I have candy." Dylan uncurls his fist. "I can give it to her."

I roll my eyes. "You're such a kid, Dyl." I remember when I offered Teeth candy.

I'm watching Dylan and counting. I estimate he has about eight days, since he has a low fever and we have no fucking meds.

I estimate Dad can last about four.

Mom probably five.

Me probably six.

Which means that, by the time he dies, he will have been functionally alone for two days already.

"I'm hungry," Dylan says.

My stomach twists. "I need to go," I tell him.

He sticks his lip out. "Where are you going?"

"Don't pout."

"Don't tell me what to do."

I figure out how to smile at him. "You're such a brat."

He smiles back.

"I'll be back soon," I say. "Gotta run an errand."

"Earring?"

"Errand."

"Oh."

I kiss his forehead. "Take care of Mom and Dad."

"I'm a kid."

"I know, I know."

I stop and throw up again on the way to the mansion. It hurts a lot this time, and I have to stay doubled over around my stomach for a minute. I can't go up there now. I need to collect myself. I turn around and go back to the dock. I don't know why I think this will help me at all.

I don't see my fishboy. He's probably under the dock again, out of the sun and out of sight. I don't think he could swim very far away right now.

Then I start panicking that someone's found him and killed him, and I have to peek under the dock to make sure he's there. He is. Asleep. Breathing.

Even if he could somehow catch a fish, he couldn't kill it. He has no teeth.

I wade into the freezing water. It cramps my calves. I have to stand still for a long time, but eventually a minnow acclimates to me. I try to channel Teeth when I grab it out of the water. It works.

The thing flops in my hand so hard I almost drop it. I don't have any good way to slit its throat, so I hit it against the dock until its neck breaks. My father told me once that it's the most humane way to kill them, but right now it feels anything but.

It stops moving instantly. I didn't expect that. I don't know. I wonder how they'll kill him.

I leave it on Fishboy's chest and start to climb out of the water, but he stirs and goes, "Rudy?"

"You better hope so," I say, with a little laugh, and he laughs too.

"Eat that," I say.

"Okay." He brings the fish to his mouth to rip it open, but it doesn't work. His face doesn't change when he starts ripping at it with his fingernails instead. I think he'll get through eventually. "I'm feeling better," he says.

"Good."

"You leaving?"

"Yeah, I have to."

"See you later?"

"Definitely. You stay here, okay?"

He nods. He got into the fish's belly good. He starts sucking it clean. There's a flyer floating in the water, drifting out to him. I'm glad he can't read.

The posters are everywhere. The Delaneys' front door is plastered. They used pictures of the Loch Ness Monster.

There's a time and a date for a hunt, and it's eight hours away, fucking Christ.

I bang on the door. "Diana, open the fuck up! *Open the fucking door!*"

She has to open the door. She has to fix this because I think she's the only one who can. I don't know how, but there has to be a way; she has to tell them she killed them or tell me I killed them because holy mother of fuck I need those motherfuckers because I cannot lose both of my boys and even if Dylan isn't really mine Teeth really is and I know that now and I cannot lose both of them when everyone has been telling me for five months that I have to stay here, that I don't have a choice, that I'm trapped on a fucking island by the fucking water and I can't leave, and I have to stay here, I have to save Teeth a million times and I have to hug Dylan, I have to love Dylan even though he's fucked and always has been and I don't know him, and I'm never going to know him, and I'm never going to know me because everyone in the world who even sees me is fucking dying, and I will never know me until I'm done knowing people who know me, and I will never ever be free.

"Answer the fucking door!"

The door swings open and there's Ms. Delaney.

I wipe my cheeks off as fast as I can.

And I have no idea what to say. With the possible exception of the fishermen, I've never been in front of an adult

I respect less, and this time, I can't be polite. I don't know if I'm ever going to be polite again.

"You're going to kill him," I say. "You and Diana, you're killing him."

She doesn't say anything.

"He's your son," I say. "He's your fucking son. He's *family*."

"You had no right coming into our lives," she said. "God knows if my daughter is ever going to be all right."

"He's your son!"

Her hand grips the doorway. "You do not know nearly enough to barge into our bus—"

"I know him!"

"So do I." And then, holy shit, she has me by the collar. "So do I. I know that boy. My little boy who could barely move. My boy who grew scales and cried in his sleep every night to go home."

I stare at her. I'm breathing so hard that my chest keeps nearly touching hers.

"He was a fish," she says. "Where would you have put a fish?" She lets go of me. "And you have a lot to learn about family, Rudy."

"He can't breathe in there. How can you pretend he belongs there?"

She looks away.

I'm getting my voice back. "He has lungs and a heart and he . . . he is just telling himself over and over again that he is all fish because that's what you wanted him to be."

"I don't regret what I did. A teenager in my doorway is not going to change that."

Then why does she cry every week on the day he was born? But she knows that. I don't need to say it.

"He's my best friend," I say.

"Considering the state of my daughter, I'd say it's better for everyone if your friends are removed from you." She glowers at me. "And you will now kindly remove yourself from my doorway."

I take a few deep breaths and back up without turning around. My head feels like it might fall off.

"By the way," she says as I'm going. "Give your brother my best." And she shuts the door.

My parents' room is dark and silent, but I can see the heap of my mother underneath the sheets. I'm still shaking and I can hear Dylan chattering on his rocking horse. I close the door. And then everything drains out of me and this quiet takes its place, heavy and hot. I don't know how my parents' room is always so warm, though I don't think I've been in here more than once or twice.

"Mom," I say.

She doesn't move, but she isn't asleep. I can tell by the way she breathes.

A loud wave hits a rock, and the house creaks. How did

we get stuck in such a shitty house? The whole place feels closer to falling apart with every single day.

But I guess we'll probably move back home soon. Which doesn't make me feel anything in the whole world.

I sit down on the bed, next to her stomach. She turns her head on the pillow to look at me. She has the same color eyes as Dylan, but hers are a lot thinner.

"Hey," she whispers. Her eyelashes are matted together.

"Hey."

She exhales for a long time.

"It's going to be okay," I tell her, because it seems like the only thing to say, and I need to say something that will make her sit up. But as soon as the words are out of my mouth, they feel mean, like I'm saying it just to hurt her. I've never been able to lie to my mother, and I don't like the squeezing in my stomach that tells me I'm doing it now.

But she doesn't laugh at me or start crying, both of which I was afraid might happen. She takes my hand and says, "I love you, baby." She runs her thumb over my knuckles.

Her fingers are smaller than mine, thin and soft. I touch her engagement ring. I've always liked it. I used to try it on, which I guess is weird. Even when I was a kid, it only fit on my pinky. The diamond is shaped like a tear. She always says that when I propose to someone, I shouldn't use a round diamond. Round diamonds are bad luck, she says.

She has spots on the back of her hands from when she was younger and she didn't wear sunscreen.

I say, "He's going to be okay."

She looks away. "I wish there were . . . God, I can't believe I'm saying this." She clears her throat for a minute. "I wish there were an easier way. A way that wouldn't be as horrible for him."

"I know." I remember learning about euthanasia in school. I thought they were talking about youth in Asia for so long. I don't know why I'm thinking about this right now. Probably because this room is so quiet. I had no idea how hard it was to hear the ocean from in here. It's much louder in my room. I wish this were my room.

I picture slamming my brother against the dock.

"Where's your father?" she asks.

"On the deck. I brought him a peanut butter sandwich." He wasn't up for much more than crying. I don't think he ate the sandwich.

He's really upset because he went out to try to catch fish today, but all he got were minnows. He can't figure out the bait for the Enkis. He tried waving a net around, and nothing. The fishermen knew something we don't.

"And your brother?"

"TV. This cartoon about a time machine. His eyes were humongous. Kid's a dork. He asked me if people can time travel in real life."

She chuckles, just a little. "I wish."

"Yeah, me too."

I don't even know where I'd go. Some time when I wasn't alive.

Because if I went back to things that I've really done, I don't know what I would do differently, which is probably such a stupid thought since everything is so fucked up. But I can't pinpoint where I went wrong. I probably didn't have to save Teeth when I found him with the fisherman that first time, but what difference did that make? He would have escaped eventually like he always did, and he would have felt like the battered war hero he wants to be. Or thought he wanted to be.

I had to save him that time he was drowning. That wasn't optional. I can't imagine standing there, watching him drown. Maybe I shouldn't have been there on the beach to see him. Maybe I should have left the house at a different time and let him just go under the water, but I can't even think about that without feeling like I can't breathe, either.

If I could go back to when Dylan was born and know how sick he was going to get, maybe I would have done something. But I don't know what I could have done. He was still just a baby. I don't know how to be a different brother. I don't know how to love him more than I do now, and that's not the heartwarming sentiment it pretends to be.

And I had to save Teeth last night. I need to accept that

and let it stay, so heavy and hard I can feel it in my mouth. Because it's true; I couldn't have let him drown in those fishermen. I didn't have a choice.

Or I did. I could have let my best friend die.

Though that would have been better. I would have lost him but saved the whole fucking island. My family would be fine. No one but me and Fiona would have noticed if the fishboy were gone. They would notice more fish and less worry.

I saved his life. I can't let that be the wrong choice.

So I make a new one; except, really, it's the same choice I've made four times since we've moved. It's that same one.

I have to save him.

I have to save both of them.

There has to be a way. I didn't die in that cave, and Dylan didn't die when he was two, and Teeth didn't die in the shrimp boat, because there is always a way. And I'm going to find it.

I'm going to be a good brother and a good friend, and maybe that means I can't be a fully good person, and I'm going to have to lie, but I'm going in. Because this time there really isn't any other choice.

"I'm going to fix this," I tell Mom.

"Just be with us, honey."

I say, "I'm going to make this okay."

She's looking at me. She doesn't want to ask.

But she whispers, "How?"

I'm about to cry, so I laugh instead, like she did. "I don't know."

She sits up and hugs me tight. My head is against her collarbone. When did she get so thin? I feel like I should be holding her and comforting her, but I just want her to hold me. I want to fold my arms into my chest so she can get her arms all the way around me, and not a bit of me will be in the open air. I don't want to be exposed to anything right now. And she lets me. She shields me with all of her. Maybe I understand more right now than I ever did.

She kisses my cheek. "Rudy. When did you get so big, huh?"

"I think recently."

"My sweet boy."

I can't focus on her. I have my plan.

The ghost is finished.

Someone can always get out, but I didn't really notice until now. Because the person isn't me.

twenty-three

HE'S UNDERNEATH THE DOCK, STILL. HE GOT A MINNOW HIMSELF, and he managed to break the neck, but this time he can't get through the skin. He's gnawing at it uselessly. I take the pocketknife I brought and slit open its belly. It doesn't bother me now.

Teeth snatches it back. "I would have shared," he says, with a bit of a grin. "You didn't have to just steal it from me."

"This is for you." I hand him the knife.

He examines it and nods. "Until my teeth grow back."

"Sure."

"Thanks, Rudy. I don't know where I'm going to put this, though . . ." He leaves it on the dock. "There."

"Not really safe there."

"When I can swim, I'll put it in my cave."

"The big cave?"

"No, too far away. I need to find a new cave. For now."

The water is up to my chest, and I'm shivering.

"You should get on the dock," he says. "It's cold under here. Even I'm cold. And I'm a fish."

I shake my head. "I'm only here for a second. I have to get back to my brother. Listen. You have to get out of here."

"Yeah, but I can't get to my cave right now. Plus it doesn't feel the same. Unless you come too?"

"No. Out of here. Away from the island."

He stares at me.

"Listen to me." I rock as a wave passes. "They know what you did. They're out for blood."

He touches his cheek.

"Yeah. Your blood. Except all of it this time."

He brings his eyes down and sucks halfheartedly at his fish. "I hate humans," he mumbles, the same way he did earlier, like he's saying something completely different.

So I say, "Me too, you know?"

He looks up.

I clear my throat. "Look. They're coming after you tonight."

"What are they gonna do?"

"Whatever they have to. They have guns, and knives,

and . . . and you won't be able to get away this time. You need to get the fuck out of here."

He's still not giving me much of anything. "And go where?"

"I don't know. Far away. Different water. Somewhere. Anywhere. And stay the fuck out of sight this time, okay, wherever you end up? No getting on the rocks to flirt with human boys, idiot."

He rolls his eyes. I want to smile.

"But I'm serious about getting away," I say. "You have to, or they're going to kill you. I mean it. They'll find you and you're not getting away this time. And I can't save you. I *can't.*"

"Why not?"

"Because there's a lot of them. A whole lot. And I'm not magic."

"You should be a fish."

"Yeah."

"Killing me isn't going to save your brother." He shakes his head. "It's not going to save any of them. They don't get that?"

"They think you're dangerous."

"I'm not going to hurt anybody!"

"I know. Teeth. I know."

He's breathing really hard and fast now. "I can't get away," he says. "Because I can't bite and I can't swim." He holds up his tail. "I can barely even kick. I can do a lap around the island, maybe. *Maybe*."

He couldn't. "I know."

He's figuring this out as he goes. "And if I swim as far as I can, that will get me out of sight, but stuck in the deep water. I'll drown. They'll kill me, or I'm going to drown."

"You're not going to drown. I'm not going to let you drown. Listen to me."

He looks at me. I've never seen his eyes this big. "I'm *really* smart, Rudy, and I can't figure out a way out of it."

"Then I must be fucking smarter, because I have this figured out. I didn't come here just to scare you to death, okay?"

"Okay." He covers his face with his hands. "Okay okay okay."

"Shh, listen to me."

"Listening." He reaches out and grabs my shoulder like he'll fall back into the water if he doesn't. I cover his hand with mine.

I say, "You're going to steal a boat. You only need to swim as far as the marina. Quietly. And haul yourself on board. You can do that. That's barely a swim. And you're out of here."

He takes a minute, drawing his bottom lip into his mouth. I'm holding my breath while I watch him. *Come on. Come on.* I figured this out. I didn't miss anything. This will work. It has to work. This is part one, and part two isn't going to work if I can't get him out of here and safe.

"Come on," I whisper to him. I grip his hand on my shoulder. The webs between his fingers are cool and smooth between mine. "You steal the boat. You sail it. Fuck, I can teach you how to sail it if I need to."

"I know how to sail." He sounds offended. "I've watched them do it a zillion times. What the fuck do you think the fishermen talk about all the time?"

"So get on that boat and get the hell out of here. Go as far as you want. Go to England. Learn the funny accent. Say 'Teeth' like it has an *f* at the end." He can't really pronounce his *th*'s anymore anyway.

"Like Madeleine?"

"No, that's France. But okay. Go to France."

He tilts his head like he's imagining this. For a second I think I have him convinced.

I hear a seagull above my head, and I smell smoke now that it's getting dark. They talked about making torches. I think they're trying to scare Teeth to death so they don't actually have to do anything. They still don't want to confront the fact that he might not be just a legend.

I don't even know why I was willing to believe I wasn't imagining him, looking back. I guess I was just as lonely as he was.

He breaks me out of my thoughts. "It'll never work."

No. It has to work. It has to work because I have to fix something, and if I have to see his body bruised and writhing and not breathing ever again, I . . .

I need to never see him again. The ghost is leaving me.

I swallow and say, "Why not? I can fix it. Whatever the reason is, I'll fix it."

He shakes his head hard, his hands creeping toward his ears. "Rudy, I can't. No no no. I can't leave the fish. I *can't*."

I was ready for this. "Yes, you can."

He keeps shaking his head, harder and harder. He's whimpering like he's in pain.

I have to fix it. "You have to leave the fish. You can leave the fish."

He's still shaking his head.

"No. Listen to what I'm saying." I take his hand off my shoulder and squeeze it as hard as I can. "Look at me. Listen to my words."

He stops moving. Completely. It's like every muscle in him is listening.

I touch his cheek because, for a minute, I absolutely have to. It's automatic.

I look right into his ugly eyes. I need to choose every word really carefully, or this isn't going to work. This is like casting a spell, but if I really knew how to do it, I would have whispered it to myself years ago.

God, I need to get this right. Today, for him.

I say, "You can leave the fish. I am standing here, telling you you can leave the fish."

He swallows. He wants to say something but he doesn't know what. "But—"

"No. You may leave the fish. You can. No one will blame you. The fish will not blame you. You have to do this. I will not look at you and think you're a bad brother. Nobody will. You have to leave because this time you have to save yourself. The fish and me, we're kicking you out."

"But—"

I hold my finger up to his lips. He flicks his eyes down to look at it.

"You're absolved," I tell him.

He brings his eyes back up to mine. There's no fucking way he knows what that word means. That's a word I dream someone will say to me.

So I put it in his language. "You're free."

There's this long minute where all I hear are the waves.

He wants to argue and say he doesn't want this. He wants to pretend this isn't exactly the opportunity he would have died for. That the real reason he needed a friend outside his family wasn't so he could hear these words.

You are no longer responsible. You are no longer allowed to give a shit. Nobody can need you ever again. Go.

All he can say is, "You'll take care of them?" His lips are chapped against my finger.

I was ready for that too. "I will."

"Promise?"

My poor fucking fishboy. "Promise."

Then he shakes his head a little, shaking my finger off. "It still won't work."

Fuck. He's used up all my reasons. "Why not?"

"'Cause boats are for humans."

I'm about to smack him across the face, I swear to God, but then he grins at me. He's kidding.

"I hate you sometimes," I say, "you know that?"

The grin slips off. "What about you?"

"Oh, I'll be fine here. They have no idea I was with you." I hadn't really realized this. "Diana didn't tell. I was in the marketplace today, and nobody knew. They're not coming after me. She didn't tell . . ."

"Saint Diana."

"Yeah."

"But I mean what about . . . you and me."

Oh.

There are a million things to say. And now I'm willing to talk about it. Maybe I always was, or maybe I can only do it because he's going away and I know I won't have to face it. But here I am wishing we'd talked about it when we had time.

Because Teeth, okay? Just . . . Teeth.

"I don't want to be alone," he says.

"Maybe . . . maybe there are more of you out there."

We both know that's bullshit. The rest of the world doesn't have magical fish. Or any miracles, really.

"Look." I take a deep breath and say the only thing that will make us both sleep tonight. "I think this is the part where we stop pretending we're not going to see each other again."

He grins even bigger. He believes me. I close my eyes and let myself believe it too, even if it's just for this second.

His voice makes me open my eyes. "I can't believe you're saving me again," he says. "I am so fucking pathetic."

"Pathetic, huh?" He learned that word from me.

"Yeah. It's like the opposite of a fish, right?"

"You got it."

He says, "But it is really whatever, you know? You've saved me way more times. And we call ourselves friends."

It doesn't matter what we call ourselves, really. "You already saved me," I say.

"That was nothing."

"I'm not talking about the cave."

He wrinkles his nose.

"That first day," I say. "When you got up on the rocks to flirt with a human boy."

He smiles big, with all his ground-down teeth shining.

I wonder if he'll do it again, with some other boy, even though I told him not to. I don't know what I want. I worry that he'll get caught again, but I can't protect him from that. I don't know if he should replace me. I know how I feel, but that's not really the point.

Once he promises, absolutely promises, that he'll be gone by nightfall, I go. I'm even colder once I leave the water. I hear him splashing around as I make my way back to the beach. He's singing quietly, this dumb fucking fishboy. Really deep inside I know I'm never going to see him again.

I come out from tucking in Dylan to find Diana standing at the shore, the handgun stretched out toward the sea. The ocean is whispering at her feet, and it must feel like nothing she's ever known, but she doesn't move. She doesn't look at all afraid.

It's been a long time since I noticed how pretty her hair is. The moonlight makes it obvious.

I stand beside her. She doesn't react.

"How did you get the gun?" I ask.

"The sheriff gave it back to my mom."

"That seems stupid."

"We know who killed the fishermen." Her voice sounds squeezed to the top of her mouth. "We don't need evidence."

"I'm surprised everyone believes you."

"People believe you when you tell the truth," she says.

"You learned that from books, huh?" My voice is so soft.

Not even quiet, just soft. I'm not thinking about the words before I say them, because I can't think of anything I could say that will matter.

Her eyes narrow. "No."

I clear my throat. I should look away from her, but I don't. I don't know. It just feels like there's nothing else to watch right now but the angry crease in her cheek. I don't feel like watching the water. It's been a long time since I looked at it without squinting for a hint of a tail.

"Thanks for not ratting me out," I say.

She doesn't say anything, just cocks her gun toward the water, swallowing.

"He's not here," I say. "He's gone."

"You helped him."

"Yeah. Why do you want to kill him?" I say.

"He killed the fishermen."

"They nearly killed him. They . . . worse than killed him."

"I know all about what they did," she says.

"I know."

"And he's not dead. He's alive."

"Bits of him." The ghost is leaving me.

"I don't want to talk about this," she says.

"You also don't want to kill your brother."

She drops the gun and looks at me, finally. She's crying. "What he did was *wrong.*"

"I know."

"How the fuck do I make sense of that?"

"I don't know."

My words thrum at my ears. I felt like this that time Teeth held my head underwater, trying to make me less afraid.

"This doesn't happen in books," she says. Her chin shakes. "There's supposed to be a right answer."

"I know."

"Can you say something helpful?"

I nod.

She waits.

"I'm sorry."

She laughs a little. It sounds so angry. "For what?"

"Being a shitty friend."

All I hear is the ocean. Then she sniffles and cocks the gun again.

If this were a fairy tale, this would be the part where the fishboy appears and Diana shoots him through the heart. Because he is a tragic hero, he's our fucking Gatsby, and he lived for his fish and he has to die for his fish. He would never let my fake authority, condoning his abandonment, making up rules about what's okay just to save his life, convince him to give up his family. He would never leave.

He would know that without him, none of us will be as good. Me, without a friend; and the fish, without a brother; and the island, without a story; and Diana, without her something real, we will all be a little bit less than we were before we knew him.

So he wouldn't leave. Not until I could come with him. And I have never been less able to leave than I am now.

But this isn't a fairy tale, and he doesn't appear. We stand here for a long time.

He really left.

Because it was all that we could do.

And I don't know if it was the right answer. But I can picture him sailing away, lonely and scared and safe. And even though this isn't the ending I want, I feel like singing when I take Diana's hand and we stare out at the empty ocean.

twenty-four

IT ONLY TAKES ME A DAY TO FIGURE OUT THE BEST FISHING spots and a couple weeks to get my technique down pat. Most everyone is still on the hunt for the fish who took the boat right out from under their noses, but every day more people give up and come here and try their hand at catching something real instead.

There are five of us regulars, though, and while the others catch a fish or two to bring home to their own families, we pool ours and divide them up and save a few a day for Tuesdays when we haul them down to the marketplace. We can just hide them under a tarp until then. Magic fish do a lot of things, but they don't spoil.

We don't make a lot of money, but it's enough for me to buy everything we need. And I usually get at least five fish a day to bring home, and that is enough.

My favorite on the team is Mr. Carlson, whose wife has MS. We trade secrets as we learn them. I was the one who figured out the bait. Well, it wasn't me, really. I knew this fish once who really liked seaweed. I just put the pieces together.

Mr. Carson and I share our seaweed. We got here earliest today, at about four-thirty this morning. I don't have much time to draw anymore. And it's too cold to think about swimming.

It's fine.

It's whatever it needs to be.

Maybe Diana will come and bring me lunch. She never has, so far, but I haven't given up hope. I still think she'll leave the house again. Someday. She can take her time. It's not like I'm going anywhere.

Sometimes I write her letters.

Sometimes I wish I cared, but mostly . . . mostly it's fine.

Mr. Carson has a huge pile already. It's been a slower day for me. "You gotta focus," he says. "Be the fish."

"Be the fish. Okay."

By the end of the day I have fifteen fish. That's enough for everyone to nod and say I did okay, but I still feel bad. I need to figure out how to rig up the net. Hand-fishing alone isn't going to cut it, but it just feels less brutal. Everyone already thinks I'm stupid because every time I catch a fish, I pause and hit it against the cliff to break its neck. "Just leave him," they all say. "They die on their own, y'know. It's not like they breathe."

"I know," I say.

Our lures bob easily in the water as we reel in our lines. The ocean has been calmer lately, almost still.

The sun is starting to go down, so I sling my basket over my shoulder and go back up to the house. Dad's always there, cooking, to grin at me when I get in. "How'd it go?"

"Eight," I say, and I smack a kiss on his cheek.

We sit down and eat together at the table. Mom and Dad and I eat bread and milk. Dylan is going on and on about this new girl with cancer who's about his age. Ever since he saw her at the marketplace a few days ago with Mom, he can't shut up about her. He thinks she's just the best thing in the world.

I smile like I'm listening, but I let myself drift off a little. I get like this in the evenings now. I stop fishing, and nothing seems real until I give everyone a weak smile good night and go up and touch the glass of my window, so cold.

And something small and insignificant inside me shatters, just like every night, and feelings hit too hard for me to stand. I bend at the waist and cling to the windowsill. I won't scream. I won't throw myself against the walls until the supports give and we fall into the ocean. I won't think about swimming as hard as I can.

No. I'll sit here with a pencil in my hand, pretending that I will draw instead of spend hours staring at a blank page. I'll think peaceful, practical thoughts about baiting hooks and making idle chatter with the townspeople.

I close my eyes and listen to the ocean.

I'm thinking about sailing, to England or maybe France. The way the wind would feel on my face and the sound of his voice screaming my name through his laughter. The waves would crash like applause. God, I remember when I used to be afraid of the ocean.

acknowledgments

As always, I'm infinitely grateful to everyone at Simon Pulse, particularly my absolutely incredible editor, Anica Rissi, and her lovely assistant, Michael Strother. That Anica continues to let me write these weird little books is one of the strangest and most awesome parts of my life.

Suzie Townsend and the crowd at FinePrint believed in *Teeth* from its inception, and John Cusick has been a very lovely stepfather to the thing. The Musers encouraged me from the start, which is quite a feat when the start in question was "I want to write a book about magic fish!" Thank you, thank you, thank you.

My incredible magic gay fish, who were named for this book and who pushed me through draft after draft, deserve metaphorical fish food galore and the world's largest metaphorical fish tank, particularly those who did reads for me. A thousand additional thank-yous to Leah, Kat, Gwen, Mikaela, Jen, Nicole, Rachel, and Erin, for loving my characters like they were their own and gently coaxing me away from many a *Supernatural* marathon when I should have been writing. Sometimes it worked. To my family, Seth, Madeleine, Alex, Galen, and Emma, for loving me.

And to everyone else I have whatevered, and to everyone else who has whatevered me.

How far is too far?

Break

by Hannah Moskowitz

THE FIRST FEELING IS EXHILARATION.

My arms hit the ground. The sound is like a mallet against a crab.

Pure fucking exhilaration.

Beside me, my skateboard is a stranded turtle on its back. The wheels shriek with each spin.

And then—oh. *Oh,* the pain.

The second feeling is pain.

Naomi's camera beeps and she makes a triumphant noise in her throat. "You *totally* got it that time," she says. "Tell me you got it."

I hold my breath for a moment until I can say, "We got it."

"You fell like a bag of mashed potatoes." Her sneakers make bubble gum smacks against the pavement on her way to me. "Just . . . splat."

So vivid, that girl.

Naomi's beside me, and her tiny hand is an ice cube on my smoldering back.

"Don't get up," she says.

I choke out a sweaty, clogged piece of laughter. "Wasn't going to, babe."

"Whoa, you're bleeding."

"Yeah, I thought so." Blood's the unfortunate side effect of a hard-core fall. I pick my head up and shake my neck, just to be sure I can. "This was a definitely a good one."

I let her roll me onto my back. My right hand stays pinned, tucked grotesquely under my arm, fingers facing back toward my elbow.

She nods. "Wrist's broken."

"Huh, you think?" I swallow. "Where's the blood?"

"Top of your forehead."

I sit up and lean against Naomi's popsicle stick of a body and wipe the blood off my forehead with my left hand. She gives me a quick squeeze around the shoulders, which is basically as affectionate as Naomi gets. She'd probably shake hands on her deathbed.

She takes off her baseball cap, brushes back her hair, and replaces the cap with the brim tilted down. "So what's the final tally, kid?"

Ow. Shit. "Hold on a second."

She waits while I pant, my head against my skinned knee. Colors explode in the back of my head. The pain's almost electric.

"Hurt a lot?" she asks.

I expand and burst in a thousand little balloons. "Remind me why I'm doing this again?"

"Shut up, you."

I manage to smile. "I know. Just kidding."

"So what hurts? Where's it coming from?"

"My brain."

She exhales, rolling her eyes. "And your brain is getting these pain signals from where, sensei?"

"Check my ankles." I raise my head and sit up, balancing on my good arm. I suck on a bloody finger and click off my helmet. The straps flap around my chin. I taste like copper and dirt.

I squint sideways into the green fluorescence of the 7-Eleven. No one inside has noticed us, but it's only a matter of time. Damn. "Hurry it up, Nom?"

She takes each of my sneakered feet by the toe and moves it carefully back and forth, side to side, up and down. I close my eyes and feel all the muscles, tendons, and bones shift perfectly.

"Anything?"

I shake my head. "They're fine."

"Just the wrist, then?"

"No. There's something else. It–it's too much pain to be just the wrist. . . . It's somewhere. . . ." I gesture weakly.

"You seriously can't tell?"

"Just give me a second."

Naomi never gets hurt. She doesn't understand. I think she's irritated until she does that nose-wrinkle. "Look, we're not talking spinal damage or something here, right? Because I'm going to feel really shitty about helping you in your little mission if you end up with spinal damage."

I kick her to demonstrate my un-paralysis.

She smiles. "Smart-ass."

I breathe in and my chest kicks. "Hey. I think it's the ribs."

Naomi pulls up my T-shirt and checks my chest. While she takes care of that, I wiggle all my fingers around, just to check. They're fine—untouched except for scrapes from the pavement. I dig a few rocks from underneath a nail.

"I'm guessing two broken ribs," she says.

"Two?"

"Yeah. Both on the right."

I nod, gulping against the third feeling—nausea.

"Jonah?"

I ignore her and struggle to distract myself. Add today to the total, and that's 2 femurs + 1 elbow + 1 collarbone + 1 foot + 4 fingers + 1 ankle + 2 toes + 1 kneecap + 1 fibula + 1 wrist + 2 ribs.

= 17 broken bones.

189 to go.

Naomi looks left to the 7-Eleven. "If we don't get out of here soon, someone's going to want to know if you're okay. And then we'll have to find another gross parking lot for next time."

"Relax. I'm not doing any more skateboard crashes."

"Oh, yeah?"

"Enough with the skateboard. We've got to be more creative next time, or your video's gonna get boring."

She makes that wicked smile. "You okay to stand?" She takes my good hand and pulls me up. My right wrist dangles off to the side like the limb of a broken marionette. I want to hold it up, but Naomi's got me in a death grip so I won't fall.

My stomach clenches. I gasp, and it kills. "Shit, Nom."

"You're okay."

"I'm gonna puke."

"Push through this. Come on. You're a big boy."

Any other time, I would tease her mercilessly for this comment. And she knows it. Damn this girl.

I'm upright, but that's about as far as I'm going to go. I lean against the grody wall of the Laundromat. "Just bring the car around. I can't walk that far."

She makes her hard-ass face. "There's nothing wrong with your legs. I'm not going to baby you."

My mouth tastes like cat litter. "Nom."

She shakes her hair and shoves down the brim of her cap. "You really do look like crap."

She always expects me to enjoy this part. She thinks a boy who likes breaking bones has to like the pain.

Yeah. Just like Indiana Jones loves those damn snakes.

I do begging eyes.

"All right," she says. "I'll get the car. Keep your ribs on."

This is Naomi's idea of funny.

She slouches off. I watch her blur into a lump of sweatshirt, baseball cap, and oversize jeans.

Shit. Feeling number four is worry. Problems carpet bomb my brain.

What am I going to tell my parents? How is this setting a good example for Jesse? What the hell am I doing in the grossest parking lot in the city on a Tuesday night?

The feeling that never comes is regret.

There's no room. Because you know you're three bones closer.

SOME GIRLS ARE ADDICTIVE.

INVINCIBLE SUMMER
BY HANNAH MOSKOWITZ

INVINCIBLE SUMMER

HANNAH MOSKOWITZ

SOME GIRLS ARE ADDICTIVE.

"ENGROSSING, MESSY, COMPLEX, AND REAL.
MOSKOWITZ'S WRITING IS RAW AND SO RIGHT."

—LAUREN STRASNICK, author of *Nothing Like You*

From
INVINCIBLE SUMMER

S he's eleven!" Noah and I protest the entire time
Melinda's patting our sister's face with powder and
dabbing lip gloss on her baby mouth. "Too young for makeup,"
I whine, and Noah drops his head onto Bella's pillow so he
can't watch. But I can't look away. Bella and I are riveted—
Bella by how old Claudia looks, me by the length of Melinda's
fingers.

"I'm only giving her a little, Chasey." Melinda traces powder over the tops of Claudia's eyes. "Making her feel just as
beautiful as she is."

Claudia's positively beaming.

"She's going to be swarmed," Noah says, his voice muffled. "Do you want her swarmed by *men?*"

Claudia laughs, all grown-up in the back of her throat. *Ha ha ha.*

"Maybe someone will fall in love with her," Bella says, and bites her lip and looks at me.

Noah looks at me, telling me it's my turn to object. "Too young to be someone's lust object," I say, then turn to Bella and mouth *Eleven,* to clarify. Bella had her makeup done before we got here, and now she's studying herself in the mirror, pinching her cheekbones and pressing the skin between her eyebrows.

"You're all too young to be talking about this love and lust shit," Noah says.

Melinda is calm, blowing extra eye shadow off her fingers. "The point is not to be loved. The point is to love." She puts on some kind of accent. "'*For there is merely bad luck in not being loved; there is misfortune in not loving.*'"

Noah picks up his head. "What's that?"

"Camus, darling." Melinda takes a book from the foot of her bunk and tosses it down to Noah. "Only the most summer-oriented philosopher in the book."

"What book?" says Bella.

Melinda examines her eyeliner pencil. "The book of life, my dear."

"Man," Claudia says. "That's one big book."

"Small font, too." Noah sits up and cracks open the paperback. "He's French?"

"*Oui*, but that's supposed to be the best translation." Melinda gathers her curly hair back in one hand and leans forward, examining Claudia's eyebrows. "You guys would like him."

Noah reads, "'*Turbulent childhood, adolescent daydreams in the drone of the bus's motor, mornings, unspoiled girls, beaches, young muscles always at the peak of their effort, evening's slight anxiety in a sixteen-year-old heart, lust for life, fame, and ever the same sky through the years, unfailing in strength and light, itself insatiable, consuming one by one over a period of months the victims stretched out in the form of crosses on the beach at the deathlike hour of noon.*'"

We're quiet.

"Well." Claudia flinches at the mascara wand. "That was happy."

"Shut up," Noah says. "I'd almost believe he grew up here."

I look at him, and I know by the way he's smiling that I'm making the same face I always make when we agree. The one that looks really shocked.

"I think it's beautiful," Bella says, quietly.

"*'No love without a little innocence,'*" Melinda recites, putting on that silly accent again.

Noah says, "Hmm," and sticks the paperback in his pocket. "All right. You kids ready to go?"

The Jolly Roger isn't much of an amusement park, and it's farther away than we'll usually stand to travel when we're down here, but every few years we all get it in our heads that we need to go. We grab Shannon and Gideon from the living room, stuff ourselves into the van, and we're off to see the creaky fun house and the carousel and the clumsy juggler.

All the windows are down and the wind sounds like someone yelling at us, but we're laughing so hard we barely hear it. The girls rake their fingers through their hair to keep the tangles out, but it's hopeless and they know it and it's okay. The lights on every restaurant, mini-golf-course, ice-cream stand, and motel rush by just like the people, who are all dressed ten times better than they ever are during the year and trying ten times less hard. I feel like we're stuck in a movie reel, roaring through as hard as we can and spinning the world into streaks.

"*'Gods of summer they were at twenty,'*" Melinda says.

It takes Noah a few minutes to find this quote in his book.

"'*Gods of summer they were at twenty by their enthusiasm for life, and they still are, deprived of all hope. I have seen two of them die. They were full of horror, but silent.*'"

Melinda takes her eyes off the road to examine us all in the rearview mirror. Claudia, for a minute, stops punching Gideon and looks at us, her artificially enlarged eyes artificially sparkling. She's beautiful—just normal, unscary beautiful—without all the makeup, but she never carries herself like she is.

"Which two?" Claudia asks.

Noah's glued back to the book. "It could be an exaggeration."

"I need to get a copy of this book," I say.

Noah nods. "You so do, Chase. And so do I. . . ."

"What's mine is yours," Melinda says softly. "As long as I eventually get it back."

We park and wait by the ticket booths, calculating how much money we have and how many rides we need to go on. I'm trying to track everyone with my eyes; I feel older than the twins but younger than Claudia, who's standing with Melinda, tossing her matted hair, while Bella and Shannon shriek and climb on each other's backs. Gideon falls down. "Everyone needs tickets," I say. "Someone has to watch—"

"I've got it." Noah gives me one of those rare, reassuring

smiles. "Melinda and I will take Gideon, okay? And you stay with Claude and the twins."

I yank Gideon off the ground and sign **Noah stay.**

Noah run Gideon says, and I try not to concentrate on that.

Stay me? Noah signs.

I realize that we never try to do anything to Gideon without asking his permission. Even though he's six, and I don't think considering a six-year-old's opinion usually comes with the territory. Some parts of being deaf are pretty sweet, I guess.

Gid spins around for a little while, then falls down again and signs **OK.**

"C'mere, you." Noah hauls Gideon onto his back and smiles at Melinda. "We've got him."

This finally hits me. "Yeah, and what are you going to do with Gideon while you're with Melinda?"

"Cover his eyes."

"Oh, ha ha," I call to their backs.

Claudia and Shannon want to ride the log flume, so we walk across the park, crunching the gravel beneath our sandals. Every few steps Bella will look at me and smile. Whenever a girl from school is nice to me like this, I'm always tripping over myself figuring out how far I'm going to try to get with her and freezing up before I can do anything. But here, I have this feeling that I can't screw this up, and there's no point in planning anything, because what's going to happen is going to happen. It's as predictable as the carousel.

She doesn't want to get splashed, so we stand under the pavilion while Shannon and Claude get in line. Bella's wearing a pink skirt, and the breeze sometimes hitches it above her knees. Her legs are starting to tan, or maybe it's that brown lotion girls use to pretend. Either way, I like it even more than I would have expected.

"Really nice night, isn't it?" she says.

"Mmm-hmm."

She revolves, looking at the lights from the Ferris wheel bouncing off the water for the paddleboats. "I love it here."

"I love everywhere here." I rub the back of my neck. "I seriously wish we could live here, even in the off-season. Like, even when it's cold, this has got to be good."

"We come down in the fall and winter sometimes. I almost like it better. No people around, everything so gray . . . It feels really old. Like you're looking at this town a hundred years ago."

"When our forefathers ran around barefoot."

She smiles at me. "Exactly."

There's no one else under the pavilion, and with the

amusement park bouncing off Bella's eyes and the dusty pink of her skirt, I can almost pretend we are a hundred years old and we know everything. When, really, the only thing I know is that I'm going to kiss her, but I'm not going to try anything more. And she's smiling because she knows it too.

It's not really that we're old so much as we've existed forever. We're in a black-and-white photo. The only color comes from the Ferris wheel lights and her skirt.

We're eternalized in the film. Forever kids. We are our forefathers today.

I kiss her, and her mouth tastes like wax and peppermint.

It's not my first kiss, but it *feels* like it. Like I'm watching a movie of my first.

She pulls back, laughing. "Chase, you bit my lip."

Or a blooper reel. "I did? Sorry."

She giggles and turns, and I smell the powder on her cheek. I want to kiss her. I want to bake cookies with her. I want to watch her put on her makeup like I got to watch Claudia.

"Look." She points to the top of the flume. "They're going down."

"Shannon looks *terrified*."

"He's just hoping Claudia will hold his hand."

We watch Claudia and Shannon take the plunge, and I wrap my fingers around Bella's palm.

"Chase."

I look up from Camus. "Shh shh shh." I jerk my head to Noah, crashed on top of his covers, shoes still on. "He's asleep. And still, for once." Noah's always waking me up by thrashing around when he's sleeping. It's the worst.

Claudia tilts from one foot to the other, doing the same little dance that Gideon does. I close the paperback and say, "You're supposed to be asleep, beautiful."

"Mom and Dad are fighting."

"Come on. Don't let that worry you."

"I couldn't sleep."

I scoot over on my bed and she sits down, her nightgown pooling around her knees. She's washed all the makeup off and she got sunburned today, so she looks like my little sister again. It's something about winters and nighttimes that makes me remember how young Claudia is. It's when she's quiet. Her voice is old; she's always confused for our mother on the phone.

"Is this Camus stuff really any good?" she asks.

"He definitely knew his summers." I flip to one of my dog-eared pages. "*Sometimes at night I would sleep open-eyed underneath a sky dripping with stars. I was alive then.'"*

She stares at me. "You can't sleep with your eyes open."

"You are so literal, Claude. Come on. Remember . . . you've got to remember. When Gid was still a baby, and Dad used to take me, you, and Noah and set us up on deck chairs on the balcony at night? Wrap us all up in sleeping bags and tell us stories? And we'd hear the waves come in and it would always be too bright to sleep—"

"Because of the stars?"

"Well, because Mom had all the lights on inside, walking Gideon up and down the hall so he'd shut up, but . . . yeah. The stars, too."

Claudia sticks her head out my window. "I mean, I don't know if they're *dripping* exactly."

"The sky's dripping."

She doesn't speak for a minute, then says, "Oh."

I tuck her under my arm and hold her for a while. She says, "I don't really remember."

"Well. You were young."

"Don't remember before Gideon." She smiles. "Was I alive then?"

"I assure you that you were."

"Your birthday's in two days."

"Oh, really? I didn't know."

She sticks out her tongue.

"Go back to bed," I say. "Gideon will feel you walking around and get all upset." Gid can tell the vibrations of our footsteps apart, and if he wakes up and realizes Claudia isn't in bed where she's supposed to be he is going to freak out. He hates when he wakes up and people aren't where they're supposed to be. Before he goes to bed every night, he takes an inventory of where we are, and if we drift, we have to be so quiet.

She kisses my cheek. "Night, Chase."

"Night."

"'*No love without a little innocence,*'" Noah says, completely still.

"I thought you were asleep. You're so creepy."

He shrugs. "So how was your lovely innocent night?"

"I kissed her."

"What a man." But he says it warmly. "How was it?"

My first thought is to relate it to soft-serve ice cream, but I can already hear Noah laughing at that. "It was nice."

"God. God, really, it was nice?" He sounds so earnest that I think for a minute that he's making fun of me. He props himself up on an elbow. "God, I fucking miss when kisses were nice. I'm so jealous of people young enough to still have nice kisses."

"Wait, kissing isn't nice anymore?"

"No. It's foreplay. Trust me, you get old enough, and everything is foreplay. Kissing is foreplay. Talking is foreplay. Holding hands is foreplay. I swear to God, Chase, I think at this point, sex would be foreplay."

This would probably be a good time to ask if he and Melinda have really slept together, but I can't make myself say the words. So I just say, "That doesn't even make sense."

"Sex is a to-do list where nothing gets crossed out."

I find the passage Melinda quoted in my Camus book. *"No love without a little innocence. Where was the innocence? Empires were tumbling down; nations and men were tearing at one another's throats; our hands were soiled. Originally innocent without knowing it, we were now guilty without meaning to be: the mystery was increasing our knowledge. This is why, O mockery, we were concerned with morality. Weak and disabled, I was dreaming of virtue!"*

Noah looks at me and coughs, his eyebrows up in his bangs.

"What?" I say.

With a straight face, he recites, *"I may not have been sure about what really did interest me, but I was absolutely sure about what didn't."*

"Come on. It's *foreplay*? Seriously?"

"You're too young." He flops backward. "You wouldn't understand. You are a fetus in a world of Camus and spermicidal lubricant."

"And you're an asshole."

"I'm just cynical. And you have no idea how far that's going to take me."

"Neither do you."

"Au contraire, little brother. I know exactly how this college game works. I will arrive, the dark horse in a band of mushy-hearted freshmen. College will pee itself in terror of my disenfranchised soul."

I roll my eyes. "Beautiful."

"Look. Listen to my words of wisdom. College's only role these days, for an upper-middle-class kid going in for a fucking liberal arts degree, is very simple. Do you know what that is?"

"A diploma. A good job. Yay."

"No. College exists only because it thrives on the hopes and dreams of the young and innocent. College is a hungry zombie here to eat your brains. It wants to remind you that your naivete is impermanent and someday, English major or no, you'll wear a suit and hate the feeling of sand between your toes."

It's not going to happen to me.

Noah continues, in a low mutter, "Like that's not already

forced into our heads every single fucking minute of every winter."

"So you're, like, essentially already educated, just because you're an asshole?"

"Because I've resigned myself to my fate, yeah. I've precolleged myself. I'm rocking the institution, entering it already all disillusioned and shit. I'm going to single-handedly change the world of higher education."

I clear my throat. *"'I may not have been sure about what really did interest me, but I was absolutely sure about what didn't.'"*

"Go to sleep. Asshole."

I never have a hard time falling asleep, but I do tonight. It takes a while of thinking of Bella's lips before I drift off.

GONE, GONE, GONE

BY HANNAH MOSKOWITZ

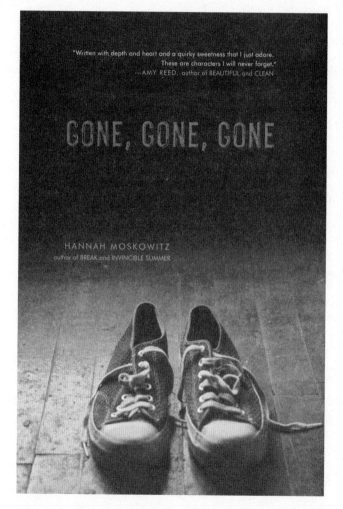

"Written with depth and heart and a quirky sweetness that I just adore.
These are characters I will never forget."
—AMY REED, author of BEAUTIFUL, CLEAN, and CRAZY

From
GONE, GONE, GONE

I WAKE UP TO A QUIET WORLD.

There's this stillness so strong that I can feel it in the hairs on the backs of my arms, and I can right away tell that this quiet is the sound of a million things and fourteen bodies not here and one boy breathing alone.

I open my eyes.

I can't believe I slept.

I sit up and swing my feet to the floor. I'm wearing my shoes, and I'm staring at them like I don't recognize them, but they're the shoes I wear all the time, these black canvas high-tops from Target. My mom bought them for me. I have that kind of mom.

I can feel how cold the tile is. I can feel it through my shoes.

I make kissing noises with my mouth. Nothing answers. My brain is telling me, my brain has been telling me for every single second since I woke up, exactly what is different, but I am not going to think it, I won't think it, because they're all just hiding or upstairs. They're not gone. The only thing in the whole world I am looking at is my shoes, because everything else is exactly how it's supposed to be, because they're not gone.

But this, this is wrong. That I'm wearing shoes. That I slept in my shoes. I think it says something about you when you don't even untie your shoes to try to go to bed. I think it's a dead giveaway that you are a zombie. If there is a line between zombie and garden-variety insomniac, that line is a shoelace.

I got the word "zombie" from my brother Todd. He calls me "zombie," sometimes, when he comes home from work at three in the morning—Todd is so old, old enough to work night shifts and drink coffee without sugar—and comes down to the basement to check on me. He walks slowly, one hand on the banister, a page of the newspaper crinkling in his hand. He won't flick on the light, just in case I'm asleep, and there I am, I'm on the couch, a cat on each of my shoulders and a man with a small penis on the TV telling me how he became a man with a big penis, and I can too. "Zombie," Todd will say softly, a hand on top of my head. "Go to sleep."

Todd has this way of being affectionate that I see but usually don't feel.

I say, "Someday I might need this."

"The penis product?"

"Yes." Maybe not. I think my glory days are behind me. I am fifteen years old, and all I have is the vague hope that, someday, someone somewhere will once again care about my penis and whether it is big or small.

The cats don't care. Neither do my four dogs, my three rabbits, my guinea pig, or even the bird I call Flamingo because he stands on one leg when he drinks, even though that isn't his real name, which is Fernando.

They don't care. And even if they did, they're not here. I can't avoid that fact any longer.

I am the vaguest of vague hopes of a deflated heart.

I look around the basement, where I sleep now. My alarm goes off, even though I'm already up. The animals should be scuffling around now that they hear I'm awake, mewing, rubbing against my legs, and whining for food. This morning, the alarm is set for five thirty for school, and my bedroom is a silent, frozen meat locker because the animals are gone.

Here's what happened, my parents explain, weary over cups of coffee, cops come and gone, all while I was asleep.

What happened is that I slept.

I slept through a break-in and a break-out, but I couldn't sleep through the quiet afterward. This has to be a metaphor for something, but I can't think, it's too quiet.

Broken window, jimmied locks. They took the upstairs TV and parts of the stereo. They left all the doors open. The house is as cold as October. The animals are gone.

It was a freak accident. Freak things happen. I should be used to that by now. Freaks freaks freaks.

Todd was the one to come home and discover the damage. My parents slept through it too. This house is too big.

I say, "But the break-in must have been hours ago."

My mother nods a bit.

I say, "Why didn't I wake up as soon as the animals escaped?"

My mom doesn't understand what I'm talking about, but this isn't making sense to me. None of it is. Break-ins aren't supposed to happen to us. We live in a nice neighborhood in a nice suburb. They're supposed to happen to other people. I am supposed to be so tied to the happiness and the comfort of those animals that I can't sleep until every single one is fed, cleaned, hugged. Maybe if I find enough flaws in this, I can make it so it never happened.

This couldn't have happened.

At night, Sandwich and Carolina and Zebra sleep down at my feet. Flamingo goes quiet as soon as I put a sheet over his cage. Peggy snuggles in between my arm and my body. Caramel won't settle down until he's tried and failed, at least four or five times, to fall asleep right on my face. Shamrock always sleeps on the couch downstairs, no matter how many times I try to settle him on the bed with me, and Marigold has a spot under the window that she really likes, but sometimes she sleeps in her kennel instead, and I can never find Michelangelo in the morning and it always scares me, but he always turns up in my laundry basket or in the box with my tapes or under the bed, or sometimes he sneaks upstairs and sleeps with Todd, and the five others sleep all on top of each other in the corner on top of the extra comforter, but I checked all of those places this morning—every single one—and they're all gone, gone, gone.

Mom always tried to open windows because of the smell, but I'd stop her because I was afraid they would escape. Every day I breathe in feathers and dander and urine so they will not escape.

My mother sometimes curls her hand into a loose fist and presses her knuckles against my cheek. When she does, I smell her lotion, always lemongrass. Todd will do something similar, but it feels different, more urgent, when he does.

The animals. They were with me when I fell asleep last night. I didn't notice I was sleeping in my shoes, and I didn't notice when they left.

This is why I need more sleep. This is how things slip through my fingers.

My head is spinning with fourteen names I didn't protect.

"We'll find them, Craig," Mom says, with a hand on the back of my head. "They were probably just scared from the noise. They'll come back."

"They should have stayed in the basement," I whisper. "Why did they run away?"

Why were a few open doors enough incentive for them to leave?

I shouldn't have fallen asleep. I suck.

"We'll put up posters, Craig, okay?" Mom says. Like she doesn't have enough to worry about and people to call—insurance companies, someone to fix the window, and her mother to assure her that being this close to D.C. really doesn't mean we're going to die. It's been thirteen months, almost, since the terrorist attacks, and we're still convinced that any mishap means someone will steer a plane into one of our buildings.

We don't say that out loud.

Usually this time in the morning, I take all the different kinds of food and I fill all the bowls. They come running, tripping over themselves, rubbing against me, nipping my face and my hands like I am the food, like I just poured myself into a bowl and offered myself to them. Then I clean the litter boxes and the cages and take the dogs out for a walk.

I can do this all really, really quickly, after a year of practice.

Mom helps, usually, and sometimes I hear her counting under her breath, or staring at one of the animals, trying to figure out if one is new—sometimes yes, sometimes no.

The deal Mom and I have is no new animals. The deal is I don't have to give them away, I don't have to see a therapist, but I can't have any more animals. I don't want a therapist because therapists are stupid, and I am not crazy.

And the truth is it's not my fault. The animals find me. A kitten behind a Dumpster, a rabbit the girl at school can't keep. A dog too old for anyone to want. I just hope they find me again now that they're gone.

Part of the deal was also that Mom got to name a few of the newer ones, which is how I ended up with a few with really girly names.

But I love them. I tell them all the time. I'll pick Hail up and cuddle him to my face in that way that makes his ears get all twitchy. I'll make loose fists and hold them up to Marigold and Jupiter's cheeks. They'll lick my knuckles. "I love you," I tell them. It's always been really easy for me to say. I've never been one of those people who can't say it.

It's October 4th. Just starting to get cold, but it gets cold fast around here.

God, I hope they're okay.

I'm up way too early now that I don't have to feed the animals, but I don't know what else to do but get dressed and get ready for school. It takes like two minutes, and now what?

about the author

Hannah Moskowitz is the author of *Break*; *Invincible Summer*; *Gone, Gone, Gone*; and the middle-grade novel *Zombie Tag*. She lives in Maryland and pretends it's the part on the ocean. Visit her at untilhannah.com.

 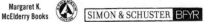